Praise For *Cha*

Charybdis is the engrossing telling of two connected stories, both of which kept me spellbound. The plots weave effortlessly between present and past. Craig-Whytock's ability to write half the novel in the formal late 1900s style of a woman's diary shows her skill as an author. This certainly is the best novel the author has written to date.

Gordon K. Jones, author of *Saving Tiberius, Predators and Prey*, and *Fighting For Decency*

Suzanne Craig-Whytock's *Charybdis* is a wonderful, powerful mystery, surely a parallel structure of two mysteries, one from the Victorian period and one set in the present day. With very strong writing, both deeply felt and entertaining. But beware, reader: there are bloody and violent twists and turns as the two mysteries tensely overlap inside of, and outside of, historical time. And yet, the reader is left with a central mystery suggested by the title: who is the true Charybdis, the true monster of Craig-Whytock's book? Remember that Charybdis was at first a beautiful girl, whom Zeus turned into a monstrous whirlpool for stealing cattle. Charybdis was a terrible danger to those, like Odysseus, who traveled by sea in the Strait of Messina. Perhaps the writer herself is the Charybdis, lurking behind, and now the reader reading, is a Charybdis, too, one with complicity in these mysteries that are, at least still partially, unresolved.

Alan Bern, co-publisher of *Lines & Faces*
and author of *IN THE PACE OF THE PATH*

Suzanne Craig-Whytock's words move seamlessly through time and space. The characters are beautifully wrought, the story riveting.

Louanne Chesney, longtime friend of the author

Suzanne Craig-Whytock does an excellent job at peeling back the onion on this mystery, leaving tidbits along the way.

Christopher Butt, author of *In The Lair Of The Kraken*

"A spellbinding Gothic tale of two women from different centuries, *Charybdis* will keep you glued to the pages. This well-written story of lives that intertwine the past and present has everything you want for a late-night read – ghosts, horror, and edge-of-your-seat suspense."

Ivanka Fear, author of *The Blue Water Mysteries* and *Jake and Mallory Thrillers*

Charybdis

A Novel

Written by
Suzanne Craig - Whytock

Charybdis

A Novel

Written by
Suzanne Craig - Whytock

First Imprint: Jane's Studio Press 2024
Book design: Jane Cornwell - www.janecornwell.co.uk
Typeset in Georgia and IM Fell DW Pica.

ISBN: 978-1-7384960-5-1
Also available in hard cover and eBook format.

Thanks to my family, and especially to my Aunt, Margaret Randall, whose poetry is such an integral part of this book.

Contents

❀ ❀ ❀

Prologue

There is no water here. It's so dry you can't even weep. Once we raised the bucket from the well just to see the full moon dancing in the water. Do you remember, Lucius?

Promise me you'll never leave me, he says.

I can't stay, I say.

But you made a vow, Louisa, he says. His face is grim.

I was six years old, I say.

And I was eight. A promise is a promise, he says. He locks the door and his heavy footsteps fade down the hallway.

Lucius is more myself than I am. I drown in him. He is the bucket and I am the moon.

At night, I dream of Charybdis, her whirlpool swirling around me and slowly devouring me. I cannot fight her anymore; instead, I beg her to take me.

Lucius returns in the morning, unlocks the door. I'm sorry,

Louisa, he says. His face is pained, like Father's face when Mother was dying. I'm sorry to have hurt you so.

I'd like some water, I say.

The well is empty, he says.

There is no water here. It's so dry, you can't shed a single tear.

Perhaps later we can go out riding, he says. Once we rode at midnight and the horses' eyes were wild in the moonlight. Your hair came loose and fell about your face like ocean waves. I could almost taste the salt in the air. Do you remember, Louisa?

No, Lucius. I choose to forget, I say.

His face is dark, like Father's face on the day he shot the old hunting hound. Lucius wanted to watch but I closed my eyes. Later, Father raised the bucket from the well and washed the blood off his hands while the moon hid its face.

He leaves me again, his footsteps thundering through the empty corridors of our lost empire. I open the windows wide to breathe in the night air, catch a whisper of dew on my tongue. The windows are not locked; they are too high above the ground to provide a means of earthly escape.

He returns at midnight.

At the crossroads where my body and soul meet, when I look for myself, I see only you, he says.

And what do I look like, Lucius? I ask. My voice is a dry husk.

Like the moon dancing in the water. I drown in you, he says. If I could have loved anything, it would have been you, Louisa.

My face is fury, like Mother's face when she realized what Father had done to the horses. With the madness of the maelstrom, I rise up and swallow him whole. Finally I am free. Finally I can drink.

GR

Part One

Chapter One: Greta

Julian was late again. It seemed to have become a habit, this disregard for her time. She twisted the ring on her finger idly, then took it off, pocketed it. Her finger felt suddenly light and a snippet from Louisa Duberger flitted through her mind: "the golden shackle on my hand." Greta quickly put the ring back on, wondering why she'd thought of that specific phrase.

She nursed her coffee on the patio, the tall heaters making the late spring cold snap bearable, trying not to check the time on her phone again. Finally, a voice behind her, cheerful and loud. "Sorry, Greta, sorry! I got tied up at work!"

She swivelled in her seat and couldn't help but laugh. Julian was out of breath, his knit scarf flying behind him as he swooped down on her like a great bird, pecking her on the cheek. He motioned the waitress over and ordered himself a coffee, called her darlin,' made the young girl giggle self-consciously. Greta frowned into her cup.

"What?" he asked, all innocence. "I was just trying to be nice."

"Well, don't try so hard," she muttered, instantly regretting the show of childish jealousy. But she'd seen him at work with the customers, especially the young female ones, prettier than her, more outgoing.

Julian's smile fell; he sat back in his chair and sighed, focused on the street instead of Greta. She regretted putting the ring back on her finger, wondered how long it would have taken him to notice she wasn't wearing it. Too late now. Besides, what if he *had* noticed? She doubted he would have addressed it—he would have ignored it like so many other things, probably speculating to himself that she'd taken it off to shower, forgotten to put it back on. Julian was infuriatingly detached, mostly due to years in the family business. His parents owned a large antique market, Trinkets And Treasures, in the heart of downtown, and they prided themselves on customer service. She'd seen Julian's father face down the rudest or most irate customers with a smile and wish them a good day, waving off any concerns Greta might have had about his feelings.

"Why don't you tell them not to come back? You don't deserve to be treated like that."

"Treated like what? People have bad days. And now he will tell his friends that he got good service."

Good service. Was that what she was getting from Julian? After all, good service was how they met three years ago. As an undergraduate, her Victorian Literature professor, Dr. Weldon, had told her about the antique market, especially about the large book section.

"Some of it's just crap, modern pulp fiction and romance,

everything tossed in together, five dollars or less. But if you spend some time, do a little digging, you might find a gem. The last time I was there, I actually got a leather-bound copy of the works of Tennyson, published in 1893. I had it appraised—I won't say how much, but...well worth the trip downtown."

She'd walked through the double glass doors of Trinkets and Treasures with anticipation, then became immediately over-whelmed. The building was cavernous, with aisles that stretched and criss-crossed like a Daedalus-style labyrinth. She stood at the head of the first aisle, wondering where to begin.

"It's a lot to take in, isn't it?" A pleasant, deep voice from behind her.

She turned. Dark eyes and a warm smile. Julian was hand-some, and tall, and the way his hair fell over one eye reminded her of the dashing heroes of Austen's novels. But which one? Was he a Darcy or a Wickham?

"It is," she replied. "I was looking for the book section."

He pointed upwards. "Second floor."

She stifled a gasp. "There's another floor?

He laughed. "Let me show you." He led her up to the vast shelves of books that took up most of the next storey. Her eyes widened and he laughed again. "Are you looking for anything spe-cific? I should warn you—none of this is in alphabetical order."

"You don't have it organized according to Dewey? Shame on you," she teased, then instantly felt regret as his broad smile wavered for a fraction of a second, barely noticeable. He didn't know what she meant, obviously, but was too polite—or self-con-scious to admit it. "No," she continued. "Just having a look. My professor recommended this place—said he'd found some good reads here."

"Professor. You're a student?"

"Literature, yes. Just finishing my degree, then onto a Master's, then PhD, hopefully."

He nodded. "Well, don't let me keep you. I hope you find a treasure or two." He strode off towards the stairs.

Had she sounded superior—had she put him off? She shrugged away the thought and reproached herself—what did it matter? They didn't even know each other. But then as he reached the top of the stairs, he called out, "If you do—find something cool, I mean—make sure you show me before you leave. Ask for Julian."

She yelled back, "I will!" It felt like a connection that was on the verge of being broken had been re-established, wasn't sure why she cared. She breathed in deeply—the air smelled musty, but it was that gorgeous must of old paper and time-worn covers. Greta loved books, loved the smell of them, the feel of them, the words leaping from the pages to form pictures in her mind. When she was a child, going to the library was a special treat. One of her earliest memories was being taken to the town library, newly built, an impressive modern structure of steel and glass. She'd been so excited that she'd pulled away from her grandfather's hand and ran forward—straight into a clear glass door. It was the only time she'd ever entered a library in tears, but the pain soon dissipated when she saw the children's reading centre, constructed like an amphitheatre, the steps carpeted to muffle the ambient sounds of patrons. How many glorious hours had she spent there, absorbed in imaginary worlds?

And how many hours did she spend in the used book section of the Trinkets and Treasures antique market? The time passed so quickly that Greta suddenly realized that she was the only patron on the second floor—it was getting close to 5 o'clock and the market would be closing soon. Three hours, three hours she'd spent blissfully unaware of the passage of time, perusing the shelves. She'd amassed a nice collection of early twentieth century children's books, a *Nancy Drew* from the fifties with a lurid cover, and she was about to take her finds down to the till to pay when she caught something out of the corner of her eye— bound in red leather, with gilt lettering, thin but beckoning. She pushed aside some Harlequin romance paperbacks and reached for the small but interesting volume nestled between them. The title on the cover was bright gold: *Idle Thoughts and Poems* by Louisa Duberger. Inside, the pages were pristine, as if the book had rarely been read despite the date on the copyright page of 1891.

The name Louisa Duberger seemed familiar although she had no recollection of studying any poet with that name. Dr. Weldon had said once in a lecture that many female Victorian writers had collections of poetry privately published—maybe Louisa Duberger was one of them. Greta would be seeing Dr. Weldon the next day; perhaps he would know more about this particular poet.

She paid for the books—there was no sign of Julian, and she didn't ask for him. Later, at home, she tossed the bag of children's books aside, made a quick dinner, and opened up the little red volume of poetry. Like a lot of Victorian verse, it was charming and observational, with a focus on daily life and nature, and even a touch of humour. The next day after class, she approached Dr. Weldon, book in hand. He looked up from his desk curiously, his bald pate glistening. His eyebrows arched when he saw what she was holding.

"Ah!" he exclaimed. "Was your expedition to Trinkets And Treasures... expeditious?" He chuckled at his own joke and Greta rolled her eyes with a smirk. "Well, let's see." He held out his hand and she deposited the book into it. Dr. Weldon examined it, his brow furrowing as he carefully turned the delicate onionskin pages. "You...you found this at the antique market?" he asked.

Confused by his reaction, Greta nodded. "Do you know who Louisa Duberger is? I've never heard of her. I did a quick internet search but the only thing I found was mention of her name in an old census."

"I'm not surprised," the professor responded, still fixated on the book. "You'd have to dig deep for information about her. She was a little-known Victorian-era poet, a recluse. She wrote mostly about death, very dark stuff, and as far as I know—at least up until now, there was only one book of poetry attributed to her, published by a company that no longer exists. And this..." he cleared his throat, "this is not it."

"Death? Dark?" Greta was surprised. "But this isn't dark—in fact, it's lovely. Cheerful even, funny. Listen." She took the book back and opened it to a piece that had made her smile the night before. "It's called 'My Garden:'

'Come to my garden, see my fused array

Of flowers. Every name you'll find.
White alyssum don the earth in snowy splendour.
Lupins tower, majestic to the sky.
Sweet peas wind their way through picket fences... '

She paused. "It goes on from there, some beautiful descriptions of flowers, then there's a humorous part at the end about pulling up the weeds. All the pieces in here are similar—imaginary landscapes full of flowers, hills, innocent longing. I really enjoyed it."

Dr. Weldon took the book back and scrutinized the copyright page. "1891? This book was published several years prior to the only collection written by Louisa Duberger that I'm aware of. That one is from 1898, called *Peruse No Epitaph Upon My Grave*, and there's only one copy as far as I know. It's in the rare book library in Toronto. She died not much later at the age of 25. And the reason we even know she was a recluse is because when the publisher shuttered, their correspondence was archived, including letters between them and Louisa Duberger—one requesting that the copy of the book be mailed to her rather than hand-delivered as she no longer accepted visitors, and another from someone, not sure who, notifying them of her death. Other than that, there's scant information about her. It's not like today, where everything one says and does is captured in the public record for anyone to 'google'—there was no 'world wide web' back in Duberger's time. The vast majority of people lived and died privately, the only reference to their existence residing in the family bible or a township census."

"At least you know more about her than I could find out," Greta said.

"At the beginning of my career, I had a colleague, a very close friend, who was studying the influence that earlier Victorian poets, like Rossetti and Browning, may have had on their later counterparts. He told me a little about Duberger, his interest piqued mainly because she was Canadian, but he hit a roadblock when, like you, he tried to pursue it." He closed the book gently and lay it on the desk. "I believe you might have something very special here."

"I think so too," Greta agreed. "The imagery is striking, especially about a place she calls 'Champs Blancs,' which I'm assuming is her home, and her voice is so positive and humorous—I'm intrigued."

"It's worth pursuing, at least as far as I'm concerned. I know you're planning on doing a Master's degree next year—I'd happily serve as your thesis advisor if you'd be interested in focusing your research on Louisa Duberger's early work. Then if you *do* decide to continue on to a PhD, you could expand into a comparison of the early and later collections. Think about it."

Greta *had* thought about it, was thinking about it during her next foray into Trinkets And Treasures, when she turned a corner and practically slammed into Julian.

"Hey!" he exclaimed in cheerful recognition. "The Literature student—nice to see you again."

"It's Greta. Greta Randall," she replied shyly. "I missed you last time—I mean, when I left. I didn't show you the book I found. A really cool poetry collection from an obscure Victorian poet. My professor thinks—"

"That it's worth a lot? Awesome!"

"No," she laughed. "That it might shed some light on what happened to her. She died very young, a recluse...alone," she clarified, seeing the confusion on his face, "and no one knows what happened in her life that caused her to hide herself away in the family mansion."

"Wow." Julian nodded, impressed. "I'm glad your trip here was worthwhile then. And I'm glad you came back. Maybe you'll find more books by her or something. And if you're still here when we close, I could take you out for a drink."

Greta was too flustered to tell him that there weren't any more books, at least not at Trinkets and Treasures. Besides, why spoil the moment? Later, she took him up on his offer, and several more offers after that, until almost three years later, they were engaged, and she was about to start her doctorate on Louisa Duberger.

And now, after almost three years, she was questioning both of those decisions.

Chapter 2: Louisa
1891

Thursday, April 2nd

Today is my birthday. I have decided to honour the occasion by keeping a diary as all young ladies must. To be more precise, it was Lucius's decision rather than mine. This diary was a gift from my dear brother, and he was quite insistent that I begin to chronicle the events of my life and my thoughts in it, so that I may "amuse him when he is bored." But I'll do no such thing. A young lady's thoughts are her own and brothers may not be privy to them, no matter how many demands they make. However, I understand that diaries are the new literature, ultimately meant for public consumption with the potential to bring about fame—or infamy!; therefore, you, the dear reader of the future, will be the only one to whom I make my confessions, and you will have to decide for yourself which parts are mere fabrication and which parts are true. But poor Lucius. His presentation of the diary was meant to be a grand gesture, but it was badly overshadowed by Father's surprise. Shall I tell you? I was astounded, as were all present, when I unwrapped a volume of poetry with my name on it. My own collection, bound in crimson leather and gilt, exactly as I had expressed a desire for this past January one night at dinner. And Father, although his clarity of mind escapes him more often lately, had not forgotten. Copies were distributed to each of the guests: Pastor Campbell, Sylvia Montgomery, who came in from town with her parents, and our neighbours the Merseys and their son Tomas (forever grateful am I that I decided not to include one of my more passionate pieces in the small volume, where Tomas may have read it and found me improper). However, I shall immortalize it here for you:

Feelings

If my libido could succumb
To its infernal passions,
My heart, perceiving such a sight
Would smoulder in the ashes.

You see? It would have been mortifying indeed if Tomas Mersey had gotten a glimpse of my 'smouldering passions.' And Lucius—he would have become even more ungenial than he was tonight after Father's gift overshadowed his own. He skulked in the corner of the parlour, refusing to join the party. I do believe that at times, I'm more the adult at eighteen than he is at twenty. He is meant to be my elder, yet often, I feel more grown up than he. And why should I not? After all, I am a professional writer now. Or at least I aspire to be, and Father's gift means so much to me that I can barely express it. I only wish Mother had been here to see it. Her recent death has been difficult for all of us, Father more than anyone—I hadn't seen him so broken since the day he was forced to shoot his hunting hound, Shadow, after she attacked Lucius. Lucius claimed that it was unprovoked, but I knew he had been teasing the poor dog until finally, she lost her

24

temper and bit him hard in the leg, an injury that still afflicts him. As he pulled the trigger, Father sobbed. I hid my eyes behind my fingers but I peeked out at Lucius. He looked...smug.

Mother's suffering was terrible and my eyes fill with tears as I think on it. Lucius was inconsolable—he locked himself in his room for three days, refusing all comfort, until the funeral. We stood side by side, and as Pastor Campbell laid Mother to rest, Lucius put his arm around my shoulder, gripping it so tightly that I winced from the pain. "You are Mother now," he whispered. "And Sister."

I was unsure how to respond and I pulled back from his grip upon me, holding my shoulder in surprise. His face became a storm and he limped away, leaving me to my grief. Later he came to me, weeping. "I am sorry, Louisa," he implored. "I never meant to hurt you. I feel so lost now. Promise me you will never leave me. Promise, as you did when we were young."

I could not deny him, seeing him in the depths of sorrow and remorse, and make the claim that I would one day depart from Champs Blancs and set up my own household, perhaps with Tomas Mersey; therefore, I acquiesced, vowing once again that we would always be together. But Lucius will find himself a wife, soon I imagine, and they will take possession of the manor. And I have no intention of being the spinster sister in the vein of Miss Austen.

Monday, April 6th

The spring has truly arrived, if the deluge of rain in the countryside is any indication. But we are grateful for the storms, as the well quite often goes dry during the summer drought, leaving us at the mercy of the river. Mabel, our housemaid, claims that she simply hates taking the buckets down to fill them up. But I believe she secretly enjoys the company of our stable hand Beechcroft, who is always the first to volunteer to accompany her in the open carriage. Perhaps they will wed... Ah, you have caught me out. I seem to be rather preoccupied with the idea of marriage today, after an afternoon visit from the Merseys and the aforementioned Tomas. They called just after luncheon. Father had gone to town with Beechcroft, so we had a lovely time sitting in the parlour and playing Old Maid while the rain pelted the windowpanes. At least it would have been a lovely time save for Lucius. He refused to partake in the game despite our invitation, and scowled each time Tomas addressed me. The young man's compliment regarding my 'charming' cameo brooch caused Lucius to clench his fists tightly—indeed, the only thing preventing him from leaping out of his shadowed corner across the card table at poor Tomas Mersey was the presence of the elders. Fortunately, Tomas and his parents were blissfully unaware of Lucius's ungentlemanly behaviour, and the three departed when the rain had stopped, but not before issuing an invitation to call on them this coming Thursday.

Once they were gone, Lucius was a fright, pacing the room and making me quite nervous, particularly in the absence of Father, whom I am sure would have tempered him.

"Who does that person presume to be?!" Lucius demanded. "He was most intimate with you, even in the presence of his own parents!"

"What on earth do you mean? Tomas Mersey is a gentleman," I responded. "You would do well to emulate him rather than being so disagreeable!"

"A gentleman!" Lucius scoffed. "I refuse to have him in the house again."

"Lucius, please stop." I was enough of a lady to keep my anger within my own heart. "You are not my guardian and the presence of Tomas Mersey in the house is not up to you. It is Father's concern. And I am certain Father would prefer me to match with someone equal to our station than to languish as a spinster. Old Maid is a card game, not something I desire to be."

Lucius put his hand over his eyes. "You ruin me, Louisa," he whispered, then he stalked out of the room, leaving me alone. I feel defeated, bereft—he has barely spoken to me this evening. For the first time, I cannot discern his thoughts. Lucius and I have always been more like twins than ordinary siblings. When we were children, we thought as one, and often finished each other's sentences, our minds were so similar. Mother always said that Lucius adored me from the moment I was born, that he took my infant hand into his own and covered it with kisses, vowing to always love his 'sissy.' As much as I find his recent behaviour strange and off-putting, he is still my beloved brother, and I hope we can make amends.

Wednesday, April 8th

The rains have continued on and off for the past several days with nothing to report save that Beechcroft drove Mabel and I to town during a dry hour. We browsed the shops and tried on hats, and then took tea at Baxter's. Of course, I was teasing when I claimed I had nothing to report. Who do you suppose we met in town, quite by accident? If you guessed Tomas Mersey and his father, you would be quite correct! Tomas was as cordial as ever, and told me he was looking forward to our visit to Mersey Hall on the morrow. And he paid me the most delightful compliment—he has read all my poems already and wishes me to write more. His exact words were, "Miss Duberger, may I be so bold as to request a poem about the spring? Something to cheer us all up?" I admit that I blushed and stuttered my reply—Mabel had the presence of mind to pull me away before I made a fool of myself.

As promised, I've spent a good portion of this evening trying to capture in words the beauty outside my window that I observed earlier in the afternoon, The clouds finally disappeared and the sky was a stunning shade of azure—it was quite breathtaking. I fear that my attempt is somewhat naïve but I will share it with you here.

To Spring

O glorious green-grass blue-sky day
You saunter through my moonshine windows
Full of winter sleep
Tossing laughter and scraps of sonnets.
Like a gasp you flow through my teeth and
O the trees with crowns of birds
The trees when they whisper of
Secret buds and far-off lands
And shadows filled with the fragrance
Of softer tomorrows.

I do hope that Tomas Mersey appreciates my efforts. The inspiration for such images is, as I said, to be found at my front door. Champs Blancs is set in a deep valley, with a remarkable view of the fields that prompted Father to bestow upon it such a name. When he purchased the property, it was in the dead of winter, and everything was covered in a blanket of white. After the fields, there is forest that grows upon the hills, and beyond the hills, the river Nith winding through the trees on the other side of our valley. When Lucius and I were younger, we used to creep to the stables at night and then ride through the forest wildly, two children with little care for the world. I was a fairy, made of light, and he was a selkie, dark and fresh from the river, both of us racing towards the dawn. The horses are all gone now, with the exception of Jack and Fancy, who pull the brougham or the open carriage. We had more, almost a full stable, but then Father had one of his turns...Mother said we must forgive Father when his mind is not his own, so I shall write no more on it.

Champs Blancs, the manor house itself, is a remarkable achievement. It was built in the early 1800s in the Revival style, with trompe l'oeil on the walls and ceilings. Father was insistent on buying it—what was the use of Mother's large dowry otherwise? he would say. It had been constructed by James Worthington, who had owned the town's flax mill. Sadly, he died with no one to inherit the property and it was put up for sale. Father was ecstatic when he discovered it—I believe I was two years of age and Lucius four when we moved here from the eastern townships. Despite the house being in a state of disrepair, it was so large—and so far below market value due to the unfortunate circumstances of the previous owner's death, that Father was overjoyed at his good fortune. The best word I can find to describe

Champs Blancs is cavernous. The ceilings are high, the rooms are large, and the corridors are long. Indeed, it is most Gothic in aspect, save for the bright and sunny parlour where I spend most afternoons, or my room which, as you have discerned, overlooks the delights of the natural world. But I must stop now—I hear the distinctive footsteps of my brother approaching in the hallway...

I am appalled and shaken by what has just occurred between Lucius and myself. His gentle knock on the door was subterfuge. Upon entering, he wasted no time. "I have decided that we shan't be visiting the Merseys tomorrow," he proclaimed, dark eyes blazing. "I will be instructing Beechcroft to send our regrets and regards first thing in the morning."

My mouth flew open and I exclaimed, "Whatever do you mean, *you* have decided? You will do no such thing, brother! I will not have you treat the Merseys with such discourtesy, and neither will Father when he returns from town!"

"Louisa!" he implored. "Do not go. Remember your vow to me, I beg of you." His voice softened. "The rain has stopped and the stars will soon appear. Come with me later to the well. We can raise the bucket and watch the moon dance in the water as we did when we were children."

As much as I despise it in myself, my heart grew cold. "No, Lucius. We will wait for Father to decide how to proceed."

He breathed in deeply and his voice caught. "As you wish, Sister. I am certain Father will be complicit in your betrayal." With that, he fled the room, leaving me torn. Lucius is more myself than I—why can he not understand that childhood oaths are simply that—things that are pledged in innocence?

Chapter 3: Greta

Greta stepped off the bus at the entrance to the university. The bus continued around the ring road, belching exhaust—she could have stayed on it, quickened the journey to Dr. Weldon's office, but it was a glorious spring morning and she preferred to walk. The campus was alive with people, all intent on enjoying the first warm day of April. As she passed the gardens by the horticulture and botany building, she could see the paperwhites were out, and the tops of tulips and daffodils had pushed their way through the soil. Soon the gardens would be a riot of changing colours, something Greta looked forward to, marking the beginnings and ends of each semester. She'd initially lived in residence during her first two years of undergraduate study and could see the gardens from her dorm window every day, but she'd taken a house with several other girls for the last four years, finishing her Bachelor's degree with one set of roommates, about to complete her Master's with another set, and saw the gardens only when she walked the ring road.

Greta had become something of a household fixture in the ramshackle bungalow on Meadow Street—other girls came and went, but Greta stayed on, mostly because of the house's proximity to public transportation. It was a good distance from the university, and run-down enough that the rent wasn't astronomical, but it was on a direct bus line that took her less than twenty minutes to arrive for class. Now that she and Julian had just become engaged, she'd finally given notice, much to the dismay of the landlord Mr. Selensky, he of the grubby undershirts and workpants, who met every request for repairs with "I'll get right on it," but who never did.

"How will I find another tenant as good as you?" he protested. "Why don't you and the boyfriend move in here? I'll cut you a deal on rent."

But Greta wanted a fresh start, a place that belonged only to her and Julian, no roommates coming and going, no sharing the bathroom with strangers. And she thought that was what Julian wanted too, although he'd been dragging his feet in the search for an apartment they could both afford, even going so far as to suggest they move in with his parents, a suggestion that Greta immediately quashed.

Today, she had no classes and walked at a more leisurely pace than usual. In fact, the only thing on her calendar for the rest of the month was her thesis defense, but even that was a formality—Dr. Weldon had already evaluated it and given her analysis of Louisa Duberger's early poetry an 'A.' As she walked, she tried to quell her nerves and steel herself for the meeting to come. How, after everything he'd done for her, could she tell Dr. Weldon that she was giving up on Louisa Duberger, abandoning the doctorate she'd been so determined to start—essentially walking away from academia?

She entered the building where his office was located, taking the stairs to the fourth floor rather than the elevator, another means of prolonging the discussion to come. Finally, a soft tap on his door, and his voice inviting her in.

"Ah, Greta!" he beamed when he saw her. "How's my favourite student? Don't tell the others I said that."

"Good, thanks." She followed his gesture and took a seat across the desk from him. They stared at each other for a moment.

"What can I do for you?" Dr. Weldon broke the silence.

"I... I need to talk to you about my PhD. I don't think I can do it." There. It had been said. Now for his reaction. Would it be anger? Shock? Disappointment? But Dr. Weldon smiled and sat back in his chair.

"Is that all? Well, of course you don't." Greta sat back in her chair too, confused. He continued, "If I had a dollar for every time I heard that exact sentiment from one of my students at the end of their M.A... you're exhausted, it's been four years of undergraduate studies, two years of the hard slog that is a Master's degree, you're no closer to solving the mystery of Louisa Duberger than you were two years ago, and you feel like giving up. Correct?"

Greta sighed. "Correct. Two years and I still know relatively nothing about her. If the plan is to uncover the reason why the tone and subject of her work changed so drastically between *Thoughts and Poems* and *Peruse No Epitaph Upon My Grave*, link them somehow, I'm at a loss."

"I understand. But I don't want you to give up just yet. Listen, before you make a final decision and walk away from what could be a great life's work, please do something for me. I know you've seen scans of some poems from *Peruse No Epitaph Upon My Grave* in preparation for your research, thanks to my 'connection' at the rare book library in Toronto. But the original, the actual volume itself, from 1898—you haven't seen it with your own eyes. I want you to go there and hold it in your white-gloved hands. Breathe in the pages. Don't breathe *on* them though—you could get in trouble; they're very delicate," he winked. "Then, after you've done that, tell me you don't want to continue your research."

Greta smiled wanly. She had her doubts, but she owed Dr. Weldon at least this one thing, and couldn't bring herself to refuse him. "All right. I'll do it for you. But I can't promise I'll change my mind."

Dr. Weldon laughed. "If nothing else, you can do some shopping while you're in the city. But I'm willing to bet that once you see her work in person, your love for Louisa will be rekindled, and we can carry on as planned. I wish I could come with you and actually see it for myself—alas, I have classes to teach and miles to go before I sleep."

Back at the house, Greta texted Julian. *"Can you talk?"* She waited for a response. After an hour, she decided to head over to Trinkets And Treasures and ask him in person if he could take some time off the next morning to drive her to the train station. With her thesis defence just days away, she wanted to honour Dr. Weldon's request and make a final decision about Louisa Duberger as quickly as she could so that she could go into the defence with a clear head.

When she walked through the doors of the antique market, it took her a minute to get used to the chaos as it always did. There were customers packing the aisles, vendors hauling carts of boxes to their booths, and a line-up at the till. She couldn't see Julian right away—then he came around the corner of one of the aisles. She waved, but he didn't notice her. He was talking to someone, laughing, and as he came closer, she realized that he was with a blonde woman, around her own age, pretty. They seemed very familiar with each other, Julian bending down to say something in the woman's ear, making her laugh knowingly. Greta slipped behind a showcase where she could watch them, knowing in her heart that she was making a mistake, that she should just approach, establish her relationship to Julian in front of the woman, instead of hiding in the shadows like a jealous lover. Then a tap on her shoulder. She jumped and turned. It was Judy, one of the long-time staff.

"Whatcha doin'?" Judy asked. "Looking for Julian?"

Greta cleared her throat, felt her face flush. "I...yeah, just looking for Julian. Have you seen him?"

Judy laughed. "He's right over there, talking to one of the new vendors." She pointed. "Gotta get back to work—it's nuts in here today!"

New vendor? Greta felt ridiculous. Julian was probably giving her the spiel, how great the money would be once customers saw what she was selling. But what *was* she selling? And was Julian buying? Greta felt immediately ashamed of such suspicious thoughts, but as if the universe wanted to prove her correct, Julian went behind the counter, then leaned over and took the woman's hand. He said something to her in a low voice. She smiled and nodded, and pulled out her phone, inputting numbers into it—Julian's, Greta assumed. She felt sick to her stomach. She fled the market without speaking to him, resolving that she would go to Toronto on her own. She could take a cab to the train station—she didn't need Julian.

When he called later, she refused to answer. She didn't have the strength to deal with what she'd seen earlier in the day, to listen to his excuses. She'd always felt insecure about their relationship—he was so larger-than-life, so social, so interesting, and she...she was the wallflower, grateful for any attention he threw her way, constantly amazed that he'd chosen her. But maybe his tastes had changed. She sent him a quick text, letting him know about the rare book library, pretended to be too tired to talk.

The next morning, Greta was up early. She'd had a restless night anyway, trying her best not to think about Julian and the blonde vendor, making herself crazy with the images that her mind insisted on torturing her with. As her cab pulled into the train station, she noticed a couple of women sitting on the asphalt outside the door. They were dressed in filthy clothes, and a shopping cart overflowing with empty bottles and bags of clothing was parked next to them. One of the women was holding a sign that read "Homeless. Every little bit helps". As the cab pulled up to the door, Greta thought she recognized one of the women, and her heart started hammering. "Can you drive around the other side to the platform?" she asked the driver. He did—she paid him quickly then got out and hurried inside the station through the platform door before the women could notice her.

On the train, she distracted herself by re-reading her Master's thesis, *Beyond The Garden Gate: Poetry and the Natural World of Louisa Duberger*. What would the thesis committee ask? She could answer anything about the work itself, but she still knew so little about the subject of her research. No one was even sure where Louisa Duberger had lived while she was writing her first collection. There were references to somewhere called Champs Blancs, but there were no clues to the specific location. And what about the gap between the first and second collections, and more importantly, what about the drastic shift in her outlook? Would holding a book in her hand really change Greta's mind, rekindle her desire to know the truth about Louisa Duberger when the truth was so exhaustingly shrouded in mystery?

After getting off the train in Toronto, she took the subway to the station closest to the library and then walked the rest of the way, grateful that the weather was so warm, and that she had thought to plan out the route in advance. She'd only been to Toronto a couple of times before, and would have been overwhelmed, gotten lost maybe, if she hadn't turned her focus away from Julian in favour of looking at street maps online.

Inside the library, she inhaled deeply. The wonderful smell of books and the muffled sound of people talking somewhere within the depths of the building filled her with calm. She asked for directions to the rare book section from a bespectacled man, who pointed her towards the stairs to the second floor.

At the desk, she waited, then a voice called out, "How can I help you?" An elderly woman emerged from a small office, smiling. "Doing a little research?"

"Yes," Greta smiled back. "My thesis advisor told me there was a copy of a poetry collection by Louisa Duberger here. Do you know it?"

"I'm familiar, yes," the woman nodded as she reached for a large binder. She flipped through the pages. "She gets checked out occasionally, although I haven't read her myself. Not very well-known, I think."

"True," Greta answered, "but she's quite interesting."

"Here," the woman pointed. "Fill in the date and your name here, then sign while I grab you some gloves. Here's a list of instructions for working with rare books. Make sure you read it carefully—these volumes are delicate."

The woman disappeared back into the office while Greta was filling in her information on the Louisa Duberger page. The librarian was correct; there wasn't much interest in the poetry collection—there were few signatures above her own. Interestingly though, the same name appeared several times: Michael Shepherd. When the librarian returned carrying the requisite cotton gloves, Greta asked, "Do you know who this person is? Michael Shepherd? Is he doing research on Louisa Duberger as well?"

The librarian shook her head. "I don't really know. He comes once in a while, takes out the book, doesn't say much."

"It would be great to meet someone who was studying her as well," Greta said wistfully. "She's a very elusive character. I'd love to bounce some ideas off another academic who might know more about her."

"I could take your name and contact information. If he comes in again, I'll pass it on to him. That's about all I can do," the librarian offered, then pointed. "Sit at the table over there and I'll bring the book to you."

Greta wrote down her contact information eagerly, hoping that Michael Shepherd, whoever he was, might be in touch. Maybe he had some new leads she could follow, she thought, then immediately stopped herself. She was getting carried away with something she had almost convinced herself she was going to put aside. Then the librarian reappeared. "Here," she said, carefully handing Greta a black leatherbound book. *Peruse No Epitaph Upon My Grave* was embossed on the front in faded gold lettering. Greta accepted it, opened the cover and stared at the frontispiece. 1898, Harris and Lambert, a publishing company now long-defunct. The epigraph was written on the next page, just as she'd seen in the scans that Professor Weldon had secured for her:

When comes the day for eschatology,

Valhalla they'll not set aside for me.

Peruse no epitaph upon my grave.

Perceive but sunken earth and crawling worms.

Such a dark and morbid introduction compared to the cheerful optimism of the earlier collection that Greta knew so well. She turned the page...and there was something that hadn't been included in the scans Dr. Weldon had procured for her—a handwritten inscription.

Chapter 4: Louisa
1891

Thursday, April 9th

Champs Blancs, which has always been a refuge, a place of comfort, is now a miserable dwelling full of strife. Father and Lucius are no longer on speaking terms and a cold silence permeates the manor. It began yesterday afternoon when Father returned from town. Lucius descended upon him in his office, demanding that he allow Beechcroft to send our regrets and cancel the visit to the Merseys. I crept downstairs and stood outside the door although I know Pastor Campbell tells us eavesdropping is a sin. Father was rightfully appalled at Lucius's discourtesy, especially on such short notice.

"The Merseys are a respectable family, Lucius. What on earth is the matter that leads you to such behaviour?' Father asked.

Lucius was silent for a moment then burst out, "Tomas Mersey was impertinent with Louisa. I won't have it!"

"He was *impertinent*? What did Louisa say?" Father demanded.

"She said nothing to me. But I have seen the way he looks at her!"

There was another pause, then Father began to chuckle. "A man may look at a woman, Lucius. Louisa is quite fetching for a girl of eighteen, and Tomas is a gentleman. If he has done nothing more than look, then I take that as a positive sign. We must do our best for Louisa, now that your mother is no longer here to advise her—"

With that, there was the violent sound of a fist hitting wood and Lucius exclaimed, "No! Louisa is mine—I mean, *my* sister. There is no need for either of us to 'do our best,' as you put it. Will you sell her off like a common whore to a man who—"

This time, Father interrupted, full of fury. "How dare you speak to me in such a way, especially about *your* sister? You do *not* have her best interests at heart if you deny her the possibility of a good match. What would you have her do? Live here forever, an old maid sitting in the corner? You will marry one day, *son*—I hope it will be soon, and your future wife will be mistress of Champs Blancs. There will be no place for Louisa here when that happens so put aside your acrimony."

Lucius muttered something in counterpoint. I could not hear it, but Father's response was disturbing and I felt dread creeping through my bones. "You will do no such thing," he said quietly. "You disgust me. Now leave."

I quickly retreated to the shadows beneath the staircase. Lucius stormed out of Father's office and swept past me, too intent on his own thoughts to notice my presence. I waited, breathless, for Father to either close the door to his office or retire to his chambers in order that I might escape to my own. After a few moments, he emerged, looking distraught and rubbing his temples with his fingers. When he reached the bottom of the stairs, he staggered and gripped the railing for support. I was on the verge of announcing myself and aiding him when he straightened and continued up to his room, leaving me bewildered. What could Lucius have said to make Father so overwrought?

This morning at breakfast, Lucius did not appear. I ate in the parlour, feeling solitary and frightened, until Father joined me, his face pale and his aspect wan. He silently accepted his plate from Mabel and instructed her to return to the kitchen to fetch him fresh coffee. When she left the room, he cleared his throat and attempted a smile. "So my dear, are you looking forward to your visit with the Merseys later today?"

I put down my teacup and looked at Father, hoping that my eyes betrayed no concerns. "Yes, I am. Tomas Mersey asked me to pen a poem about spring for him. I am anxious to hear his thoughts on it."

Father nodded. "I'm certain he will enjoy it, my dear. Sadly..."

I held my breath. Had Lucius convinced Father after all? But he continued, "Sadly, Lucius and I will be unable to accompany you. Beechcroft will drive you in the brougham and Mabel will act as chaperone, so you may not be disappointed."

As he spoke, Mabel returned from the kitchen. While Father was putting the sugar in his coffee, I let my breath out slowly. "Thank you, Father. I will be sure to convey your regards to the Merseys. But are you unwell?"

"Just a slight headache, my dear. Nothing to concern yourself with."

After breakfast, Mabel helped me choose a dress, and pinned up my hair. Mabel was only three years my senior, but she was a sensible person, and I knew Mother would have been satisfied with her acting as chaperone under the circumstances.

We arrived at the Merseys mid-afternoon, and Tomas was the first to greet us, causing me to flush ever so slightly when he asked right away about the poem. I had inscribed it in my best hand on parchment and had tied it with a red ribbon. He was delighted, and read it out loud to his parents once we were seated in their parlour, remarking on how vivid the images were.

All in all, it was a lovely afternoon. Mrs. Mersey was most attentive, questioning me about my writing, and offering to accompany me to town the next week so that we might visit the dressmaker's before the Spring Ball at Hampton House. "It will be your proper introduction into society," she stated. "And you simply *must* have a new dress, I'm sure your father will agree."

Beechcroft arrived promptly at 4 and as we prepared to depart, the most incredible thing happened. While his parents were saying farewell to Mabel, Tomas approached. "I hope you will save a dance for me at the Spring Ball, Miss Duberger," he said quietly, and then he held up the red ribbon that I had used to secure the poem. "I will hold this dear to my heart until we meet again." Before I could respond, Mabel ushered me to the brougham and we rode away. I confided in Mabel that Tomas had asked for a dance at the Spring Ball, and she clapped her hands with enthusiasm. Mabel agrees with me that Tomas is handsome and good-natured, and that his keeping of the ribbon is a very positive sign.

Friday, April 10th

My pleasure over yesterday's visit has been dampened by the continuing animosity between Lucius and Father. Lucius did not appear at dinner last night nor at breakfast again this morning; when I questioned Father as to his whereabouts, his face hardened. "Your brother is... indisposed," he answered, with a kind of finality that led me to understand I should pursue it no further. I plan to spend the day writing, although I take little pleasure in those things that inspired me even just last week. How quickly life can change. The joy I felt on my birthday has turned to despair, and I question my intentions regarding Tomas Mersey. If the mere suggestion of a possible match between us can cause such a rift between Lucius and Father, is it not perhaps better to abandon the scheme altogether? Until now, Lucius and I have never had a wrong word between us—our love for each other was absolute. I cannot begin to understand what drives his jealousy, although I know with Mother's death, he has become more reliant upon me for comfort when he has one of his darker moments. As children, he demanded my complete attention; if I played with any of my dolls for too long and neglected him, he would snatch it from my hands and pull off the arms or tear out the hair. Then, when he saw how upset I was, he would weep and beg me to forgive him.

"You made a vow, Louisa," he would cry. "Never leave me. You know I will die if you do!"

Always the vow. Lucius's fixation on the words of innocent

children may unravel any hope of happiness I might attain.

Tuesday, April 14th

Mrs. Mersey called for me today as promised and we drove to town in their very spacious and luxurious landau. We made conversation on the way and I learned that she and Mr. Mersey have been happily wed for almost twenty-five years, that he made his fortune in flax, and that he plans to transfer the mill to Tomas two years hence and retire. She suggested, quite boldly I thought, that overseeing the daily operations of a busy mill was a time-consuming business and that her hope for Tomas was that he should find himself a cheerful and capable wife to run the household at Mersey Hall. I believe she gave me a pointed look when she made the statement. I dare not pin my hopes on it; yet Mersey Hall is a fine house and I should be proud to be mistress there. I only hope Tomas might agree.

At the dress shop, Mrs. Mersey was most helpful in picking out a lavender tulle that she said would complement my eyes. I became emotional and spent a few moments among the hats composing myself; these are the things I imagined Mother and I doing together, that she would have taken charge of my coming out. I miss her greatly at times like this and endeavour to remember her the way she was before she wasted away from illness. Mrs. Mersey seemed to sense my sadness and diverted me by modelling a gentleman's top hat, much to the amusement of everyone in the shop.

But then, when we had finished making our selections of fabric and finery, and the fittings had been completed, the most embarrassing thing occurred. I told the seamstress to put my purchases on the family account. She opened her account book, perused it for a moment, then quietly informed me that the family account was overdrawn. I was mortified, but Mrs. Mersey stepped in and said, "Put all these purchases on my account today." When I protested, she smiled and replied emphatically, "You were so hospitable to us when we last called on you that I simply must return the courtesy!" I was confounded by the lack of funds in the family account; the only reason for it, as I explained to Mrs. Mersey, is that Father had become so absent-minded after Mother's death that he simply forgot to pay the balance. Mrs. Mersey agreed that must be the case and reiterated that she was happy to ensure I was properly introduced in a tulle gown, as my own mother would have done.

Her kindness continued when we returned back to Champs Blancs in the landau, as she invited me for tea after church this coming Sunday. The Spring Ball, hosted by Mr. John Zehr and his new bride Felicity, is in a mere two weeks, and my excitement can barely be contained. My first ball, and already with the promise of a dance with a most eligible bachelor, one whose mother seems to have taken a liking to me. If only Lucius and Father can resolve their differences, and Lucius can promise to get along with the Merseys, I would be the most happy girl in the province. My fondest wish is that Lucius will also meet someone, kind and proper, who might take my place as the object of his affections, so that I may be free of our strange sibling bond. I'm quite certain that other brothers do not take such exception to the possibility of a sister becoming betrothed, especially when it is to someone of an equal station who can provide for her so well. But Lucius has always possessed a fixated mind. When we were young and visited other families with children our age, he would refuse to play, choosing instead to hide in a corner reading a book, entreating me to hide with him rather than share my attention with anyone else. He would often be teased, the others finding him in his corner and whispering cruel insults like "Lobcock" at him, leaving me to defend him where he would steadfastly refuse to defend himself. I love Lucius with all my heart; he is my brother, but at times, my most fervent desire is to be separate from him. At times I feel him overpower me, that when I gaze into a mirror, his face is the reflection; when I speak, his voice spills over my lips and breaks my teeth. And that is why I hide this diary from him. If he knew the truth, he would be crushed.

Chapter 5: Greta

"Well? What did it say? Don't leave me in suspense!" Dr. Weldon exclaimed. Greta had made an appointment to see her professor as soon as she'd gotten back from Toronto, and now they were sitting in his office on a gloomy Wednesday afternoon, drizzle dripping down the windowpanes and casting whirling shadows on the bookshelves lining the walls.

"It wasn't much, but it was interesting. 'To Louis: Perhaps someday.' Here," she said, taking a page out of her tote bag. "I was able to use one of their overhead digital scanners to capture it." She showed Dr. Weldon the scan. The handwriting was faint, but elegant and feathery, with the upper-case letters looping in a fanciful way. "Do you have any idea if Louisa Duberger knew anyone called Louis?"

"No," the professor mused, staring at the scan. "It *could* be someone she knew. Or it could be that the book was given as a gift from someone else who'd purchased it for this 'Louis,' and Louisa Duberger had nothing to do with it. The plot thickens."

"The publishing house, Harris and Lambert, wasn't a large

company, at least as far as I could find out. And I don't think this book would have been bought by a stranger, do you? I mean, Louisa wasn't very well-known, wasn't known at all really, outside a very small circle, so would Harris and Lambert have been a small local publisher, printing limited runs? Like a Victorian vanity press? Which leads me to think that if Louisa had all the copies and gave them out as gifts...," she paused.

"Then this could be an inscription penned by Duberger herself, to the enigmatic Louis," Dr. Weldon continued. "But of course, it doesn't matter much since you're not continuing your research." The twinkle in his eye belied the seriousness of his tone.

Greta cleared her throat. "Actually, I've been giving it some thought. I'd really *like* to continue but I need to figure out finances first. It looks like I might be carrying the cost of an apartment on my own moving forward, and my current teaching assistantship is finished at the end of the summer semester, so I have to see whether I can juggle both a job and school."

Dr. Weldon sat back in his chair. "I was under the impression that you were engaged. Are you and the other young person not planning on cohabitating? Not that it's any of my business."

"No, it's okay. He and I are...taking some time." She didn't tell Dr. Weldon that right before their meeting, she and Julian had had a terrible argument. He'd been calling her all day, and she'd let it go to voicemail, avoiding the inevitable. Finally, she couldn't take the incessant notifications and increasingly anxious texts, so she'd called him back.

"Thank god," he said, relieved. "I was so worried about you!

What have you been doing? I've been calling and messaging all last night and all morning—why didn't you answer?"

"I've been busy," Greta had responded mildly. "Sorry."

"Judy said you came by the market on Monday, but I didn't see you."

"I saw *you*," she answered. It was hard to keep her voice calm after two days of torturing herself with sordid images of Julian and the blonde woman.

"Well, why didn't you say anything?" He sounded confused.

"You looked... busy. You had your hands rather full. I didn't catch her name," Greta said sharply.

"I had my 'hands full'? What are you talking about? Wait— are you talking about Sierra?"

Greta snorted. Of course it would be 'Sierra.' "Oh, was that her name? The two of you looked like you didn't want to be interrupted. As she was taking down your number, I mean."

Julian let out a sudden gasping laugh. "Greta, are you kidding me?! Is that why you haven't been returning my calls? She's a new vendor and I was walking her through how she could log into the online sales site to see her daily sales reports. What exactly did you think you saw?"

"You were *holding her hand*!" Greta was beginning to feel overcome with emotion, something she hated.

"Because she sells jewelry! And she was showing me a ring that she wanted to put in a showcase. Damn, Greta—what's going on with you? How could you think that I was—what, cheating on you with some antique market vendor?"

Greta felt sick. "I'm sorry. It just looked like—"

"I can't believe you don't trust me. That really hurts, Greta."

"I said I was sorry. But you've been so distant lately, and it seems like you've been actively avoiding any conversation about getting a place together and I just worry. You *know* that."

Julian sighed. "I haven't wanted to talk about it because *I'm* worried. About money. And I *do* know how much you get in your own head, but I thought we were past that. Listen...this is a lot right now, and it's really busy here. I need to go."

"Can we talk later? Come by the house and I can make you dinner. Please." She was on the verge of crying. Julian always sounded so reasonable when she questioned him about anything, and now all she felt was incredibly stupid for making accusations.

"I don't know," he said. "Maybe it's better if we give it some time, calm down. I gotta go." Then he hung up on her.

She'd been beating herself up the rest of the afternoon, clenching her fists on the bus over to the university, berating herself for her lack of confidence, her suspicions, and most of all, for making Julian feel as though she had no faith in their relationship. And now, sitting in front of Dr. Weldon, she did her best not to burst into tears.

"Taking some time?" the professor repeated. "Well, that's not always a bad thing. Better to be safe than sorry. But listen—if finances are what's holding you back, I have an idea."

Greta perked up. "What idea?"

"I have the funding to hire a research student beginning in September. The pay is pretty good—your tuition would be covered as well as additional expenses. And I'm assuming you're going to apply for research grants?" Greta nodded. "Then money shouldn't be an issue. Use me as a reference for any grant proposals and I'll put in a good word for you."

Greta sagged back in her chair. "That—that's amazing. How can I ever thank you?"

"Solve the mystery of Louisa Duberger and we'll call it even."

Greta left Dr. Weldon's office feeling elated. Her first instinct was to call Julian, tell him the exciting news, then her heart dropped when she remembered how they had left things between them. And as badly as she wanted to see him, to run to him and feel the safety of his arms, she knew she needed to give him some space. She'd texted him right after he'd hung up, apologizing profusely, and she could see that he'd read the message, but he still hadn't responded.

She stopped at the grocery store, picking up a few things to make a nice dinner in case Julian changed his mind. When her phone rang just as she was unpacking the groceries in the small kitchen she shared with the other girls, she dropped the head of romaine she was carrying and grabbed the phone in a panic. But it wasn't Julian—it was her sister. She sighed when she saw the caller ID and let it ring one more time before answering, preparing herself for the conversation ahead. Helen never called unless she wanted something. Money usually, and twice, bail. When they were little, their grandfather had dubbed them 'Greta Garbo' after the actress, and 'Hell On Wheels.' The names had stuck and seemed to have played a part in forming their very different personalities. As the older sibling by five years, Greta did her best to protect Helen, practically raising her from the time she was old enough to change a diaper. Their mother, Tammy, was an alcoholic and drug addict, in and out of rehab for years, leaving the girls with their grandparents, at least when she thought to mention that she would be gone. The absence of a mother figure made Greta more responsible; it made Helen more reckless. By thirteen, she'd been arrested for shoplifting. By fifteen, her first abortion, the father a neighbour in his thirties who fled town before the police could find him. At seventeen, she'd already been in rehab herself once. Greta still fumed when she remembered the day that Helen had come home from the rehab clinic and she and their mother had shared 'war stories.' Greta had realized long ago that, as much as she loved her sister, or at least tried to, Helen was their mother's daughter through and through: impulsive, thoughtless, and narcissistic.

"Hey, Helen. What's up?" Greta tried to sound upbeat, dreading the response.

"You're not going to *believe* the shit that's been happening!" her sister began.

Greta inwardly winced, ready for the worst. "Oh no, what's wrong?" She tried to be sympathetic as Helen raged on about her current boyfriend, Arion, a forty-year-old unemployed welder. Greta had assumed, correctly, that the welder was not, in fact, unemployed, but that he was a drug dealer, which Helen was currently confirming.

"And now he says he's kicking me out because I won't sell for him! What the hell—he knows I'm on probation! Can I come stay with you? Please!"

Greta breathed in deeply. "I'm really sorry, Helen. There's no room here, you know that."

"But I can sleep on the floor—I don't care! I've slept in worse places. C'mon, Greta, please."

Greta didn't know what to say, so she said nothing. The silence grew. Finally, Helen snapped, "You know what? Fuck you, Greta." She hung up. Greta stood in the middle of the kitchen, still holding the phone tight in her fist. A line from Louisa Duberger leapt into her mind: *Images of castles fill the air/ Then just dust, dust, dust.* That was how her life seemed to her right now—everything she'd hoped for, turned to dust.

Family? Dust.

Friends? Dust.

Julian? Dust.

When would the water come and wash it all away? She imagined herself as a whirlpool, swirling and sucking all the horrible days into herself, and then spitting them out, destroying them and everything else around her.

She walked over slowly and picked up the romaine. She contemplated it for a moment, turning it one way and another, then hurled it at the wall. She stood, fists clenched, breathing hard, then from behind her, a voice. "Damn. What did that lettuce ever do to you?"

She turned around, saw Julian standing there and started sobbing. He held out his arms to her and she moved forward into them, just as she'd imagined earlier. When she'd finally calmed down, she said, "I'm sorry. I honestly am."

Julian held her at arm's length, studying her face. He wiped a tear from her cheek and touched his finger to his tongue. "Salty. Just like you."

Greta laughed. "Stop holding hands with strange women and I'll stop being a dumbass."

"Deal. But does that mean I can't hold your hand anymore? I mean, you *are* kind of strange—" He stepped back in mock-protest as she slapped his arm. "Feisty too! But I know what will make you feel better—why don't I make dinner? I hope you like tossed salad."

Greta rolled her eyes and picked up the romaine. "You'll need to give it a thorough wash—I can't vouch for this floor."

She handed the lettuce to Julian and went to the refrigerator to take out the chicken she'd bought. Scanning the shelves to see what other ingredients she had on hand, she said, "I thought I saw my mother the other day."

Julian was shocked. "Seriously? Where?"

"Outside the train station. Begging people for money with one of her druggie friends. I feel shitty about it but I went in the other door."

"It's not shitty. You know what would have happened if you'd stopped to talk to her, let alone given her money. No wonder you've been on edge."

"Yeah...I'm sure I did the right thing but I still feel guilty." Greta spied a block of cheese hiding behind the milk jug. "Do you want to do parmigiana or—" Her phone rang again, the shrill sound breaking the calm of the kitchen. "Damn it!"

"What's wrong?" Julian asked, as she looked at the screen.

"First Tammy, now Helen. She called a little while ago. She's in trouble again," she answered, sighing with frustration. But it wasn't Helen, calling back with new demands. The caller ID simply said 'Unknown.'

"Hello?" she answered tentatively.

"Hi there. Is this Greta Randall?"

"Yes. Who's this?"

"My name's Michael Shepherd. The librarian at the rare book library gave me your contact information. I hope you don't mind me calling so late, but I was wondering if you'd like to meet. I have some information about Louisa Duberger that might interest you."

Chapter 6: Louisa
1891

Finally, the day of the Spring Ball has arrived. Sadly, my enthusiasm stands in stark counterpoint to Lucius's grim demeanor. My dress, the one made of the beautiful lavender tulle with a silk slip, chosen by Mrs. Mersey, arrived yesterday. I put it on to show Father and Lucius; Father was delighted but Lucius's eyes opened wide in shock and his expression became strange. While Father complimented me and expressed his gratitude to Mrs. Mersey for her excellent choice, Lucius was silent. I said, "Come, Lucius, what is your opinion? Is it not the most beautiful gown?"

He exhaled sharply and announced, "The neckline is too low. Your... bosoms are exposed."

Father tutted at his remark and I laughed, much to Lucius's discomfiture. "What do you mean? My bosoms are well under the protection of this fine tulle and silk. And the neckline is exactly as it should be—this is the *style* now, Lucius." His scowl deepened when I enquired about the evening wear he himself had chosen for the event, at which point he announced that he would not be attending "such a tedious affair" and would rather stay home.

"You will do no such thing," Father commanded. "It will do you good to be in company, especially with so many of the town's young ladies in attendance, any one of whom might make a suitable wife. You will soon be one-and-twenty—high time you commence the search for a mistress for Champs Blancs." This displeased Lucius and he stalked away to the library, where he stayed most of the evening. I refuse to let his dour disposition spoil the excitement of my first ball. Mabel is coming to help me dress and pin up my hair, after which we shall depart for Hampton House.

Saturday, May 2nd

The Spring Ball is over and it was a beautiful dream that slowly became a nightmare. Lucius attended with us, albeit grudgingly, but he cut quite a dashing figure in his dress coat and tie, and Father looked very distinguished as well. When we arrived at Hampton House, we were greeted by Mr. and Mrs. Zehr, and joined the rest of the guests. Despite the longing gazes of several young ladies directed towards him, Lucius refused to mingle and proceeded directly to a corner where he could glower at everyone. Father immediately made his way to the lounge where he found comfortable seating. He still seems to be suffering from a great fatigue but waved off my concerns and suggested I take a turn around the room in search of Sylvia Montgomery, the daughter of our friends from town and my elder by one year. I discovered her quickly and she was as pleased to see me as I was her. No sooner had we greeted each other when the Merseys arrived.

From across the reception hall, Tomas was scanning the room, and when our eyes met, he smiled and made a speedy approach.

"Miss Duberger, Miss Montgomery," he greeted us, and almost immediately followed with, "The band will soon begin playing. Remember you promised me a dance, Miss Duberger." I nodded happily and presented my dance card and pencil, upon which he placed his name in the first spot, as well as in two others. He was about to re-join his parents when he turned back and said, most formally, "Forgive me, Miss Montgomery for my oversight. May I also have the pleasure of a dance with you?" Sylvia held out her own dance card; Tomas entered his name and then quickly withdrew, glancing back over his shoulder at me.

Rather than being offended, Sylvia was quite amused and remarked that I seemed to have captured the attention of the most eligible bachelor at the Spring Ball. I coloured and attempted a response, but she took my arm and said knowingly, "It is a most perfect match. I wish you the best. And I am sure Mr. George Barton will be affronted when he sees that his name is not the only one on *my* dance card!"

We took refreshments while waiting for the dancing to begin, and there was a pleasant atmosphere in the hall, with the guests merrily eating, drinking, and chattering together, when suddenly there was a disruption and everyone turned to look. To my horror, it was Lucius, in a confrontation with Tomas Mersey! He was yelling something unintelligible and Tomas was attempting to calm him. Father appeared; he took Lucius roughly by the arm and pulled him away, speaking sharply to him. Lucius then stormed out, leaving Hampton House and abandoning us to public ridicule. All eyes turned to me, and Sylvia backed away under the scrutiny, as the attendees began murmuring their displeasure at Lucius's lack of etiquette. I stood, alone in my humiliation, until Mrs. Mersey broke free of the crowd and came to my rescue. She took my arm and led me to the refreshment table, as the band struck up and the rest of the crowd moved towards the stairs leading to the ballroom.

"What happened?" I asked her, abashed. "What did my brother say to Tomas?"

Mrs. Mersey looked uncomfortable. "Apparently he is unhappy with my son's attentions towards you." She relinquished her hold on my arm as Father approached. "Perhaps it would be better if your father took you and your brother home."

It was a devastating experience, made worse on the journey back to Champs Blancs by Father and Lucius's bitter silence towards each other. Finally, we reached the house and once we were out of earshot of both Beechcroft and Mabel, Father exploded in anger. "How dare you disgrace this family with your outrageous behaviour?" he demanded.

"*My* behaviour?!" Lucius countered. "Tomas Mersey is to blame for this! He—"

"Has done nothing wrong, brother!" I interjected. "You have ruined my relationship with the Merseys as well as *any* chance of happiness I may have had. I'm going to my chambers."

They renewed their argument upon my departure, so I stood outside the door for a moment as the battle raged. "I told you once before to put that outlandish notion about Louisa out of your head. She will *not* remain at Champs Blancs with you, a spinter to your bachelor—or worse!"

I was at a loss to think what Father meant by 'worse'; there could be nothing worse than spending the rest of my days wandering the hallways of Champs Blancs like a lonely spirit, with only a brother to keep me company.

Later, I was preparing for bed when there was a knock at my door. It was Lucius. "Please, Louisa," he entreated. "Let me in."

"No," I responded harshly through the oaken panel. "I cannot bear to look at you. You have crushed my hopes and made a fool of me."

There was a long pause. I could hear him breathing raggedly. Finally, he spoke, his voice choked. "And you have destroyed me." His footsteps faded down the hallway, and I finished getting ready for bed. It was hours before I could sleep—Mrs. Mersey was too much a lady to be cruel in the moment, but I knew that she could no longer possibly entertain a match between me and Tomas. An overdrawn family account is one thing; public embarrassment by an intemperate brother is an entirely different matter.

Sunday, May 3rd

I have sequestered myself in my room since Friday evening, refusing to see Lucius, emerging only when he went out riding and then fleeing back to my chambers as soon as I heard his footsteps in the main foyer. I spent some hours well into the night contemplating writing a letter to the Merseys on Lucius's behalf without his knowledge, a profuse apology that might serve to smooth the waters between us all—Lucius and I had the same tutor and our handwriting is virtually indistinguishable—but I know that if he found out, I could not predict what he might do, and it strikes me with terror. I finally fell asleep this morning as the sun was rising, only to awaken a few hours later, too heart-sick to attend church. My attempts to write have been in vain, as my thoughts are in turmoil, and the only verse I could conjure was this quatrain that seems to capture my sadness:

> *A bed of roses always comes*
> *With thorns that pierce unwary thumbs,*
> *And weeds appear to choke a flower,*
> *The sun is lost behind a shower.*

When Mabel came with my luncheon, she informed me that Lucius was once again out of the house. I took advantage of his absence and wandered the corridors of Champs Blancs, wrapped in a shawl to ward off the chill that seems to have seeped into my bones. It is now late in the afternoon. Father has taken to his bed with a headache, and Mabel has prepared a poultice for him. I pray this is not the beginning of another of his 'turns.' He is my only ally and I dread to think what might happen to me if Father succumbs to another brain fever. If he is no better on the mor-row, I will petition Lucius to fetch Dr. Bain, and if he will not, I will make the journey myself.

Monday, May 4th

Father has taken a turn for the worse and he rages with feverish delirium. Mabel is frightened, as am I. I was finally able to bring myself to speak with Lucius—he came into the parlour where I was eating a hasty lunch before returning to Father's bedside. When I asked him about Dr. Bain, he laughed dismissively, as if the events of the last few days had not even occurred. "You worry too much, sister. Father will recover without intervention as he has done in the past." Then he went out to the stables, leaving me to tend to Father. Mabel and I will do our best to bring down the fever, but our medical knowledge is limited.

🛐 🛐 🛐

It is now late in the evening. I am truly horrified at the latest events and have no one to turn to. Late in the afternoon, Father's breathing became shallow and his skin grew cold. I sought Mabel but could not find her anywhere. I begged Lucius to bring Dr. Bain, but again he refused. "I will fetch him myself then!" I declared, and this infuriated my brother.

"You will do no such thing! You may not roam the country-side unaccompanied," he decreed.

"Then Mabel will come with me—Beechcroft can drive us in the carriage." I made to leave, to ask Beechcroft to prepare the horses, but Lucius put out his arm and detained me.

"Sadly, dear sister, with Father being bedridden, I felt the need to determine the state of our finances. It was an unpleasant surprise. Father has been a spendthrift, wasting money on lux-uries and trivialities and now we are close to destitute. I had no choice. I have released Mabel from her earthly duties, and she has departed. But don't worry—I gave her a very good...reference."

He laughed again, a cold, sneering sound, so different from the brother I knew and loved that my blood froze.

"What do you mean, Lucius? You had no right!" I protested.

"I have every right!" he roared back, looming over me like a bird of prey. "With Father incapacitated, I am the man of the house, and I may do what I wish in his stead!"

"Father would not have wished any of this," I said quietly, my voice trembling. "You know that, brother." I turned to leave, to go back to Father, but again he stopped me.

"Go to your room, Louisa. There's no need to fuss over Father. I'm sure he will be fine. But if it makes you more content, I will stay with him."

Tears filled my eyes. Lucius's face softened and he reached out to stroke my cheek. I pulled away from his touch, and his dark eyes flashed with renewed animosity. "Go to your room," he ordered again, and I fled to my chambers. It is now evening, and my room is dark. I have not yet dared to venture out, fearful of coming across Lucius, but hunger is my new motivator. With Mabel gone, I need to investigate the stores of food in the kitchen and make inventory.

Strange. I found the kitchen in disarray as if Mabel had left in the middle of preparing the evening meal, and her outdoor boots are still by the back door. She must have been overcome by the shock of Lucius terminating her position in the household. Fortunately, I found the pantry full, and collected some cheese and bread for a light supper. As I was returning to my room, Lucius came upon me. When he saw the food, he pleaded with me to join him in the parlour and share a meal with him. "There are still apples in the cellar. We can have a feast under the table by candlelight as we did when we were children. Won't that be fun, Louisa?"

I shook my head, words escaping me, and returned to the silence of my room. I heard his footsteps pacing outside in the hallway but he did not knock—finally, he left me in peace. After finishing my meagre meal, I realized that my water jug was empty. I picked it up, intending to fill it from the well, but when I turned the handle of my chamber door, it was locked. Lucius has imprisoned me.

Chapter 7: Greta

"Are you sure you don't want me to come with you?" Julian asked, as Greta was putting her laptop into its bag.

Greta smiled. Ever since their big argument, and the subsequent make-up session that seemed to have breathed new life into their relationship, Julian had been very attentive, taking her out for a romantic dinner and surprising her after class with flowers, much to the delight of the students in her tutorial group. "No, I'm sure. You have a lot to do today with—how many new vendors are coming in?"

"Six. But don't worry. None of them are young and blonde," he teased, and she threw a sock at him. "I'm just concerned about this Michael Shepherd guy. I mean, you don't know anything about him. Like *nothing*."

"I'm certain it'll be fine. Even though it seemed like he was being deliberately vague when I was trying to get him to explain what his connection to Louisa Duberger is, I can't believe he's some kind of stalker type. Maybe he just doesn't like talking on the phone." Greta stuffed some pajamas into her overnight bag and zipped it closed.

"Well, promise me you won't go with him anywhere dark and dangerous. You're meeting at Spinoli's?"

"Yep. Totally public—I'll ask for a table right in the middle of the restaurant. And my hotel is a two-minute walk up the street. The very public street. Honestly, don't worry. I'll text you as soon as I'm finished meeting with him, and we can talk after I get back to the hotel."

Julian seemed satisfied, although he waited with her on the platform at the train station until it was time to board. Then he hugged her tightly and kissed her, whispering, "Don't run off with this guy just because he's Louisa's long-lost cousin or something."

Greta laughed and climbed the steps into the train, looking back at him. How could she have doubted him for a moment? She found her seat—she had deliberately requested a window seat—and waved to catch Julian's attention. He waved back and started towards the parking lot as the train pulled out of the station. As he got near his car though, a young woman approached him and said something to him. Greta craned her neck to try and keep the pair in view but the train picked up speed and she lost sight of him. Who was the woman? How did Julian know her? Greta stopped herself, remembering that she had promised not to let her mind spin out of control with destructive thoughts about Julian, deciding instead to reread some of the poems in *Peruse No Epitaph Upon My Grave*.

There was one piece in particular that she kept going back to, called *A Broken Life*. It was a dark and disturbing contrast to the lightness and beauty of Duberger's first collection. The last three stanzas in particular made Greta feel tremendous empathy for Louisa:

What can a shell that walks around,
Oblivious of all human sound,
Offer a world that sits in wait,
For someone to appreciate?

I'm lost within this tangled web,
That grasps and chokes – not long I'm dead.
So bitter world, to you I give,
My place for someone else to live,

To read my words and hear my voice
And know I never had a choice
For all I saw, and all I spoke
My life is buried under oak.

Greta thought about Louisa, so young, probably around the same age as Greta herself, but in the depths of such deep despair that she wrote poetry about being trapped and longing for death, a shell of a person. And what could have caused it? Was she alone, no family or friends to support her? What a terrible thing for a young woman to feel that isolated, especially in a time period where there wasn't much else to do but be 'in society.' Greta hoped that Michael Shepherd might have some answers that would not only help with her research but shed some light on Louisa. She had to admit that she'd grown attached to the poet—at least attached to the idea of her, this girl who used to write about spring and flowers but now represented everything

Greta imagined a lost soul to be. It was almost gothic—in fact, if Louisa Duberger had been writing a few decades earlier, perhaps she could have been another Mary Shelley or a Brontë, rather than an obscure poet whose life story was hidden in time. But Greta, despite her initial misgivings, was determined to raise Louisa Duberger out of that obscurity—if she could.

The rest of the trip passed by quickly, and after checking into her hotel, she had a little time to kill before dinner with Michael Shepherd. She was nervous—what if he really was a crackpot? He'd said he was in Toronto spending a couple of days at the library, but she wished he'd wanted to meet somewhere closer to home. Some people jumped at the chance to spend time in the city, but Greta wasn't that adventurous by nature. She quelled her uneasiness by wandering down Yonge Street and window shopping, until she came across a second-hand store called Prufrock And Co. Intrigued by the name, and assuming it was a reference to one of her favourite modern poets, T.S. Eliot, she went inside. Shelves of tchotchkes lined the walls and racks of vintage clothing stood on either side of the antique wooden counter. A middle-aged woman was behind the counter, examining the bottom of a piece of pottery with a magnifying glass. When she heard the door chime, she looked up.

"Hi there. Are you looking for anything special today or just having a browse?"

"Oh, just browsing for now, thanks," Greta answered. She scanned the shelves aimlessly, then had a sudden brainstorm. "Actually, do you have any old clocks? My fiancé collects these little windup clocks from the 1950s."

The woman thought for a minute then walked over to a shelf

near the back of the store. "Like this?" she asked, producing a small brass clock with two bells on top. "It's a West German Meister Anker double bell alarm clock from around 1953."

Greta took it from her and examined it. It was exactly the kind of thing that Julian loved; ironic, because he was so into technology—he was continually upgrading the store's computer inventory system and even built his own gaming computer by himself, ordering all the components online. "This is perfect," she told the store clerk. "How much is it?"

"$48.00. But," she added hastily, "it's in really good condition and it works—if you don't mind the ticking, that is."

"I'll take it. The price is fine," Greta reassured her, thinking that it was actually a lot, but Julian deserved to be splurged on. "He's going to love it."

The store clerk wrapped the clock for her, and Greta tucked it away in her bag, then checked her phone for the time, glad that she didn't have to rely on a wind-up clock to tell her she needed to get to the restaurant.

Spinoli's was around the corner from the second-hand store and she arrived with a few minutes to spare. After giving her name, the hostess said, "Oh, your friend is already here. Right this way."

Greta was burning with curiosity as she followed the hostess through the restaurant, searching for tables with a single male occupant, until finally they stopped at a booth against the back wall. The man seated at it was reading something on his phone;

when he realized that Greta and the hostess were standing in front of him, he quickly put the phone away and leapt up, smiling. "Enjoy your meal," the hostess said, placing two menus and a wine list on the table, then she left the two of them alone.

There was a long pause, during which Greta began to worry that the hostess had taken her to the wrong table. "Uh, are you Michael?" Greta asked. He was tall and thin, middle-aged, with dark graying hair, and laugh lines around his blue eyes and mouth. He reminded Greta of someone, maybe an actor, but she couldn't quite remember which one.

"I am. And you must be Greta. So happy to meet you." His voice was deep, with the slightest hint of an accent.

"Same," Greta said as they took their seats. "I've been very excited to speak with you! About the information you said you had?" Michael didn't respond—he just kept smiling. "Here," he said, passing her a menu, then opening his own, scanning it. "The polenta fries are supposed to be very good, and the pasta carbonara too, so I'm told."

Greta studied the menu, hoping that he would be less recalcitrant to begin discussing Louisa Duberger after they'd ordered drinks, worried too that her enthusiasm had maybe put him off. Michael insisted on choosing an expensive bottle of Bordeaux, after reassuring her that the meal was his treat, despite her protests. "It's not every day that I get to meet someone who's as interested in Louisa Duberger as I am."

"So how did you become interested in her?" Greta asked, taking advantage of the opening.

Michael took a slow sip of his wine. "Mm. Well, she's actually my great-grandfather's aunt, so my great-great...great-aunt? I suppose."

Greta's jaw dropped. "You're...related to her?"

"Very distantly, yes. I'd never heard of her before—she and her family had left the eastern townships in Quebec and moved to Ontario in the 1870s, but she came to stay with my great-grand-father's family near Montreal for a brief time in the 1890s, not long before she died. Okay, your turn. Why are you interested in her? The librarian who gave me your contact information said you were doing research—for what?"

"I did my Master's thesis on her first volume of poetry after finding a copy in an antique market, believe it or not. Then, when I started digging deeper, I read some of her later work and... became fascinated, I guess. I'm about to start my doctorate on her."

Now it was Michael's turn to look surprised. "Really? That's amazing! I'd love to read your thesis. Even though she's a part of the family, I don't know a lot about her. To be perfectly honest, I only learned about her when my father developed Alzheimer's. He used to tell me stories about his childhood, and could conjure up memories of his father and grandfather as if it was just yesterday, but he couldn't remember my mother's name, didn't even know who *I* was by the end."

"I'm so sorry to hear that," Greta said.

"It's all right—eventually he just slipped away painlessly. But my father said that great-grandpa Louis was really taken with Louisa, that she was a poet, and his favourite aunt. She died when he was very young, of course, but she visited on more than one occasion and he described her as 'beautiful and sad'".

"Wait—did you say your great-grandfather was named 'Louis'?" Greta felt on the verge of a revelation, about to discover the identity of the mysterious Louis from the inscription, but they were interrupted by the waiter. Greta ordered her meal, impatient to resume the conversation, but Michael became sidetracked by the arrival of bread and garlic butter. Finally, the waiter left and the bread was buttered, leaving Greta still breathlessly waiting for an answer.

"Louis?" she prompted. "That was your great-grandfather's name? The inscription in the poetry collection at the rare book library is made out to a 'Louis.'"

"Indeed," Michael answered, swallowing the last of his bread. "I assume that the inscription refers to him, although I have no idea how that book ended up in the rare book library instead of in the *family* library."

"And what does it mean, 'Perhaps one day'?" Greta asked, hoping Michael would know the answer.

Michael shook his head. "No clue. She passed away when he was only around seven years old. My father always talked about her being a poet, so I did a little research of my own and found a copy of her first book, the one you have. I became a bit...obsessed with her, I guess you could say, and went to the rare book library a few years ago, looking for more information. The librarian, the one you met, found me that copy of *Peruse No Epitaph*. I've been going regularly, visiting it, you might say, the way one would visit a relative. I feel very connected to Louisa—something in the DNA, I would imagine. And then of course, two years ago, I took over her family home."

Greta sat back in her chair, in awe. "You live in Louisa Duberger's house?"

"I do," Michael said with a grin. "And you won't believe what I found there."

Chapter 8: Louisa
1891

Tuesday, May 5ᵗʰ

Father is dead, I know it. He must be; otherwise, how could he allow Lucius to keep me captive as he does? I spent last evening calling, then hammering on my chamber door, pleading with Lucius to release me until my voice was hoarse, and my hands badly bruised. There was no response, no pity from my brother, and finally I fell into a fitful sleep. I'm thankful that I had the foresight to bring the cheese and bread from the pantry back to my room—I've rationed well and it has sustained me, but I have a terrible thirst, not only for water but for freedom. I opened my window earlier and breathed in the cool night air, but there was not a drop of dew to be had. I will wait for Lucius to return to the hallway and then beg him for a jug of water. He cannot refuse me if he loves me as much as he claims. I am simply bewildered by his actions, and fearful of what may come next. And Father. What has become of him? Has Lucius left him to grow cold in his bed without the ministrations of Pastor Campbell? I grow heartsick when I think of it, yet I cannot grieve until I am certain of his fate. Perhaps he is on the mend but too weak to leave his room.

It has grown dark and still no word from Lucius, no sign of his presence outside my door. I hear stirrings in the farthest reaches of the house, but cannot say what he could possibly be doing. I am faint from both hunger and thirst—does he plan to deprive me of sustenance until I perish? I cannot reconcile this stranger, this cruel master whose derangement knows no bounds, with the brother I loved so much as a child.

Right before dusk, as I was writing down my thoughts, I heard footsteps approaching. Weeks ago, not long after Lucius presented me with the diary, I secured a hiding spot for it by prying up a loose floorboard beneath my bed. As the footsteps grew nearer, I quickly secreted the diary and prepared myself should Lucius enter. He did. Quietly and carrying a pitcher of water. I leapt to my feet and demanded that he release me.

"Why, Lucius? Why are you keeping me a prisoner in my own room? I need to see Father!" I exhorted him. But it was of no use. He remained detached, holding the pitcher close to his chest. "Lucius! Answer me," I demanded. "Someone will surely come, and you will have to explain your actions!"

"Who will come? Mabel is gone and Beechcroft would never dare venture into the house. The Merseys will not forget the events of the ball, nor will Tomas have any interest in a girl whose family has lost its fortune." He paused then sighed. "Forgive me, Louisa. You must be very thirsty. I would happily give you some water, but the well is dry." He tipped the pitcher over and I blenched at the thought of such a waste, but nothing poured forth.

"How is this possible? I do not believe it!" I declared. "It rained most of the spring—the cistern must still be full at least. And what about Father? Is he to wither away from thirst as well due to your cruelty? Please, Lucius—let me see him. If you love me, let me go to him." I sank onto the bed, my head in my hands, but Lucius was unmoved. Finally, I lifted my head and met his eyes. "What do you want of me? Tell me, that I may do it."

"What do I want? I have told you so many times, Louisa, in my letters, letters that I never had the courage to give you until now." He put down the empty pitcher and came closer, pulling a packet of folded papers from his pocket. "I want us to be together always. Here," he said, passing me the packet. "Read these and tell me you do not feel the same."

I took it from him reluctantly, unfolding the sheets of paper and reading through them silently, the horror of what he was suggesting within them growing with each word, filling me with dread.

"You see, Louisa? We can be as we were when we were children, when we played Father and Mother. You are Mother now and I—I am Father."

I could no longer contain myself, and threw the letters onto the bed. "Lucius! What have you done?!"

"What any man might do, Louisa. You are mine. Father is gone, and we must carry on. You will stay with me—I want us to be together always." He knelt before me, eyes pleading, and he took my hand in his own.

"Lucius," I said quietly, trying not to recoil from his touch. "I need to go. I cannot become what you imagine me to be." He began to breathe harshly, gripping my hand so tightly that I cried out in pain.

"Then you shall never leave," he stated flatly, releasing me and walking out of the room without a backwards glance.

I fell to the floor and pounded the oaken floorboards with my bruised fists, my despair overshadowing the pain. How could this be real? How could someone I have known since I came into this world, the one person whose side I always took, to whom I always gave my fullest love and attention, treat me in such a way? It was truly not to be believed. And Father? Gone? Did Lucius expedite his passing?! I crawled into my bed and curled up, keening like a wild animal caught in a trap.

Wednesday, May 6th

I wept without tears and wandered my room until well past midnight, stifling the screams in my throat. Finally, I distracted myself from grief by scouring the bookshelves for something comforting. I chose Homer's *Odyssey*, one of Father's favourites, remembering how he would read the tales of Odysseus and his adventures, delighting us by taking on the voices of each character in turn. When the last of the candle burned away, the wax pooling around the cherubs at the base of its intricate bronze holder, I fell asleep with the book in my lap, and dreamed of Scylla and Charybdis, the mythical monsters that Odysseus was forced to choose between. I am not unlike Odysseus now, facing two different types of imprisonment but with no Circe to guide me. I either crash against the rocks of my own mortality or get sucked into the madness of the maelstrom. The window beckons and I stare out across the beautiful fields that once inspired me, but which are now beyond my reach. I cannot think. My mouth is dry and my lips burn. I feel a delirium coming over me and I open the window to make my escape...

I find myself on the floor beneath the window, having swooned from weakness, and wake in the throes of a feverish hallucination. I laugh hysterically and begin to spin around the room like a gyre, waving my arms and swirling my petticoats like a madwoman. I am the whirlpool, I *am* Charybdis, and I leap across the bed as if it was the Straits of Messina, determined to destroy the interlopers who dare to sail between I and my sister, Scylla. I crash to the floor and lie still, panting with exhaustion. I reach my hand above my head, and then I touch something strange, something still warm but unmoving. I roll over and onto my knees and scream. Lucius is lying there, his blood draining into the floorboards, his skull shattered by the heavy bronze candlestick holder and then I remember with sickening clarity that he came to my room in the night, raving and drunk, demanding what he called his "rightful due" and he forced me onto the bed and I screamed but he covered my mouth and stole what virtue I had left and when he was finished, he sat up on the bed with his back to me, his shoulders shaking, begging my forgiveness, and I reached over and grasped the bronze candlestick holder, the carved cherubs on its stem slicing into my palm, and I whirled around like a maelstrom and brought it down as hard as I could onto his head.

He collapsed without a sound and dropped to the floor, silent, lifeless, the blood seeping from his skull to stain the oaken planks. I fell next to him, staring into his still-open eyes, this brother whom I had once loved now turned into a monster that I abhorred. And once again, it was a terrible truth that Lucius and I were the same because now *I* was the monster. I lay there for what must have been several hours, insensible, unknowing, until the sun began to rise and shook me out of my stupor, the thirst burning in the back of my throat compelling me. The door to my room had been unlocked and I ran down to the kitchen, using the last of my strength to power the water faucet, pumping the handle up and down frantically. If I could have, I would have burst into tears at the sight of the water flowing freely from the tap and I thrust my face underneath the stream, gulping down the sweet cool water until I was finally satiated. Then I remembered Father—if Lucius had lied about the well going dry, could there be a chance that Father still lived? I grabbed a pitcher from the cupboard and hastily filled it to the brim. I ran back up the stairs, leaving a trail of water behind me, and threw open the door of Father's room.

"I'm here, Father!" I cried, but even from the doorway, I knew I would receive no response. It was too late. I approached the bed slowly—his skin was green and his jaw was slack. My heart filled with fury as I stared at him, lying there, having died alone. Did he ask for me? What deceptions did Lucius tell him? Did he pass into the next life believing that I had forsaken him? My body was overcome with cold, and I began to shake uncontrollably. I sank to my knees and cried out in pain and anger, not knowing what to do. I couldn't simply leave Father in his bed to rot, nor could Lucius remain on the floor of my chamber, his blood drying and staining the oak.

I found a warm shawl hanging in the kitchen, and went out to the stables. I called for Beechcroft but there was no response—had he left with Mabel? Despite his absence, I was still quite capable of saddling my own horse. I would take Fancy and ride to...but where would I ride? How could I disclose the events of the past few days to anyone? Who would believe me? No. I could not open myself to scrutiny, and risk being condemned for both Father and Lucius's deaths. I reached the stable at any rate, intending to feed the poor horses, doubting that Lucius had taken pains to ensure their well-being either. I opened the door and my nostrils were assailed with a rank odor—metallic and sharp. The walls of the stable were splashed with something dark and the floor was slick. Moving forward, not hearing the familiar nickering that normally greeted me, my heart in my throat, I peered around the door of Jack's stall. The gelding lay on his side, his throat opened and gaping. I ran to Fancy's stall; she had met the same hideous fate. I backed away and almost tripped. I looked down. To my horror and disbelief, it was Beechcroft. He was prone on the floor of an empty stall, his lifeless leg preventing the door from sliding closed, the early morning sun glinting off a farrier's blade protruding from his chest. Behind him, as if thrown carelessly away, Mabel lay in a heap in the corner. The wounds on her neck were dark and livid—she had been throttled to death.

I gagged and retched up all the water that had so recently quenched my thirst, then flew out of the barn. I could not bear to see any more death. I sat in the dirt on the ground next to the well and stayed there for what must have been hours, my mind shattered, unaware of the setting sun. When the moon rose, I emerged from my trance. I stood and stared down into the well. The moon was full—I could see its reflection shimmering in the distant depths. As children, Lucius and I had taken such great delight in watching the moon dance in the water. Oh, how I longed to return to those innocent days when I was the moon, an unknowing prisoner of the well, but Lucius has laid waste to our happiness, his obsession consuming everything. Now he will rest where we once rejoiced, imprisoned forever while I am finally free.

Chapter 9: Greta

"Letters?" Greta asked, astonished. This could be the break she was waiting for, she told herself, the first clue towards solving the mystery of Louisa. "You found letters? From who? *To* who?"

"I don't know," Michael said mildly, pouring himself another glass of wine. They'd finished dinner, a delicious meal of pasta carbonara and salad. Greta had declined dessert, anxious to find out what Michael had discovered in the house that was so intriguing it necessitated a full meal first.

The buzz of the restaurant seemed to amplify as Greta waited for him to elaborate. He didn't. Greta tapped the table with her index finger impatiently, but he didn't take the cue. She decided that maybe he was an introvert and needed to be encouraged to talk, so she followed up with, "Why don't you know?"

"There's no signature and no real salutation. They all begin 'To the one who chains my soul' and end with 'The one who lives in torment.'"

"That sounds so dramatic. What are the letters about? I could probably take a guess—a man who's in love with a woman who doesn't love him?"

"That's the gist of most of them. According to what I read, the two of them had known each other from the time they were children. Lots of flashbacks to things they did together when they were growing up, Christmases spent together, things like that."

"Cousins maybe?" Greta mused. "Although, marrying your cousin had fallen out of favour by the mid-1800s. Maybe they weren't related but lived in the same house, like someone who worked for the family?"

"Not sure. Apparently, they spent a lot of time in the saddle," Michael said.

Greta laughed. "Do you mean...?"

Michael hesitated, looked confused. "They did a lot of riding—on horses." He was so deadpan that Greta flushed slightly, embarrassed at her assumption that he was speaking euphemistically. Michael didn't seem to notice, and continued, "And here's the best part—in some of the letters, there are references to 'the one who chains my soul' being a poet."

"A poet? Then it *must* be Louisa Duberger! That might be a clue to who the mysterious would-be lover is."

"Maybe, but I don't recall my father mentioning that Louisa had ever married, or was even engaged. Of course, great-grandpa Louis only knew her when she visited Quebec. She wasn't even twenty the first time she came, and he hadn't been born yet. I don't think he ever got a chance to travel to see her in Ontario before she died. And of course, that side of the family had no money left—the house, Champs Blancs, went to the bank as far as I know, when Louisa passed away. It was a huge place, derelict, cost a fortune to keep up, and from what I understand, her father had frittered all the money away. There were no immediate heirs, and no one in my family wanted it. I was extremely lucky to find it after all this time. Most of the land has been parcelled out, but I still have about twenty acres. Very private—you could almost say 'hidden away.'"

"And where did you discover the letters? I can't believe no one else had seen them before now."

"They were in the attic, hidden in a dead space between the wall and the joists. I'd gone in to check because it smelled like something had died up there. I got poking around, and there they were." Michael gestured at the bottle of wine. Greta shook her head, no, and he drained it into his glass. "From the paper and the handwriting, I'd definitely say late 1800s, but I'm not an expert. He was really fixated on her—'Oh L., living without you would destroy me,' things like that. Obsessive."

Greta was taken aback. "What do you mean, 'L'? I thought you said the letters didn't specify to whom they were written. 'L' could definitely be Louisa."

Michael paused, then cleared his throat and waved his hand dismissively. "Oh, didn't I mention that before? At any rate, it's a logical assumption to make. I mean, the fact that the letters are written to a poet, it was her house...all of it."

That made sense to Greta, who had been worried for a brief moment that Michael wasn't telling her everything—he certainly seemed like a bit of a control freak. But then again, what motivation would he have to lie to her? "Okay, so if the poet referred to in the letters *is* Louisa Duberger, it would fit with the timeline. But who could the mysterious and obsessed letter writer be? I keep coming back to someone who lived in the house. From what I understand about the time period, girls were pretty cloistered…" A sudden thought popped into Greta's mind and she grimaced. "Ugh. What if it was her father or something? That would explain why the letters were hidden."

"Doubtful. Most of the references to the past involve your 'would-be lover' as a child at the same time as the 'object of desire,'" Michael countered. "Anyway, I haven't made a thorough search of the place yet—it was only when I found the letters that I thought maybe I was onto something, that I could learn more about Louisa. To tell you the truth, I find her fascinating."

Greta smiled. "Me too. So much so that I've devoted the last two years of my life to her, and probably the next five. I'm so happy that we were able to meet. It's like…kismet or something, that we both happened to frequent the same library."

Michael was quiet for a moment, nursing his glass. Then he tossed back the contents and stared at her. "Do you know," he said, slurring slightly. "I have an idea."

Greta stared back. His eyes were slightly glazed and she was a little concerned about what he might say next. "What idea?" she asked hesitantly.

"Well, I have plenty of room. At Champs Blancs, I mean. Why don't you come for a visit, help me look for more clues? You're in Waterloo, right? It's not that far—I could pick you up and then you could stay for a couple of days—wait!" he exclaimed, seeing the wary look on her face. "I don't mean…I don't intend anything inappropriate. But imagine—we could scour the house and maybe find some more letters, something that could help you in your research and me in—well, in just finding out more about my family. I'm the only child of only children on both sides and sometimes I just feel a little lost, without any links to the past—or the present. Think about it, will you? A published PhD thesis, all about my great-great…how many greats is it again? Anyway, that kind of positive recognition about Aunt Louisa would be so wonderful!"

Greta paused, feeling a certain kinship with him. She understood what it was like to be alone in the world, especially after the deaths of her grandparents—even though she had a sister and a mother, she didn't feel any familial connection to either of them. "Maybe," she said slowly. "But I'd have to check with my fiancé first. Make sure he was all right with it." Greta knew for certain that Julian was confident enough that he wouldn't have an issue with it, but she wanted Michael to understand that there was someone looking out for her. Just in case.

"Oh, of course! Of course you need to check with your fiancé! Why don't you ask him, and then let me know. Here. I'll give you my email address and we can touch base later. I'm sure you're dying to see those letters. And I can't wait to show you the house. Imagine the insights you could lend to your research after immersing yourself in the place where so much of her writing was set."

Greta put his email into her phone, and after a few more minutes, she said goodnight. Michael insisted on calling her a cab, even though her hotel was only a couple of blocks away. "It's dark, and you never know who's prowling around," he said, as she closed the cab door and waved. It didn't occur to her until later that it was strange that he hadn't brought at least one of the letters with him. But maybe he was worried about them getting damaged or something.

Once she was back at her hotel and settled in for the night, she called Julian. She was looking forward to teasing him about the gift she'd gotten him. Greta was a terrible gift-giver—she couldn't keep a secret to save her life, and usually told him what she'd bought him for Christmas or his birthday the second after she'd paid for it. The phone rang a few times then went to voicemail. She left a message, trying to sound upbeat instead of worried about where he might be. Maybe he'd had to stay late at work— but what could he be doing there *this* late?

She put the tv on to occupy her mind, hoping that Julian had been in the shower and had missed her call, that her phone would ring any second and it would be him. But an hour later, she still hadn't heard from him. She texted—"Where are you right now? I'm back at the hotel"—and then waited to see if he was reading the message. He did, right away, and then she waited. She could tell that he was typing but it seemed to take forever for his response to appear.

"Just out getting groceries—call you soon." Greta breathed a sigh of relief and then became angry at herself. What was wrong with her? Julian was her fiancé—he wasn't out gallivanting with other women. Why couldn't she trust him? She knew she had abandonment issues, thanks to her mother, but she really needed to give Julian the benefit of the doubt rather than running the risk of sabotaging their relationship—again.

The hotel room was beautifully decorated with floral wallpaper reminiscent of a William Morris design and the furniture was lush and comfortable. The bed was a four-poster, king-sized, and Greta stretched out, imagining herself in another time and place, thinking about Louisa Duberger, wondering what Michael's house was like, and whether Louisa's bedroom was the same as when she'd lived there. Probably not—styles changed so much over the years that the owners would have redecorated, maybe even remodelled Champs Blancs until it barely resembled the house Louisa had grown up in. Still, to spend some time in Louisa's actual home would be an incredible opportunity. 'Champs Blancs,' she thought. Such a lovely name. Her long disused high school French told her it meant 'White Fields.' She was pondering the origin of the name when her phone rang. She grabbed it and answered immediately.

"Hey, how did it go?" Julian's voice on the other end was soothingly familiar.

"Good, I guess. He's a little strange. Getting him to talk about anything was like pulling teeth. He certainly likes to play coy."

"So what was the big intrigue? What information did he have?"

Greta launched into a full recount of the dinner, and the letters. "I get the feeling he's not telling me everything," she finished.

"Why?" Julian asked. "What do you think he was holding back?"

"I don't know. Maybe he was just trying to keep me interested.

I think he might be lonely."

"Makes sense," Julian agreed. "You *are* pretty hot."

"Don't be ridiculous!" she protested. "I'm sure his interest is purely academic. Besides, he knows we're engaged."

"Well, good. I hope you also told him your fiancé is very tall and works out. But listen," Julian changed the subject. "What does this guy do that he could afford such a huge house—Champs Blancs, you said he called it—and that much property? Is he rich? I mean, only rich people name their houses—he must work in tech or something. Oh, maybe he's the CEO of some big company."

"He actually never said, and I didn't think to ask. As for the house, I guess it's always been called Champs Blancs, even though it's a bit of a wreck now. In fact, that's how he found it, he said. He was driving around in the area, trying to 'reconnect with his roots,' and he saw a faded old sign at the end of a laneway. He followed the road back until he came to the house. When he saw it, he couldn't believe it. He knocked on the door and spoke to the old couple who lived there. He said they were just rattling around inside like two peas in a giant pod, and they were more than happy for him to take it off their hands. They weren't even using the upstairs, were basically confined to the kitchen and a couple of rooms on the main floor.

"He just waltzed in and bought the place? Just like that? Wow." Julian sounded as amazed as Greta was when Michael told her the story at dinner.

"You know," she broached the topic hesitantly, "he's invited me to go to the house, to see the letters for myself. What do you think?"

There was a long pause. "I don't know, Greta. The whole thing sounds weird. What if he's...like, a serial killer or something?"

Greta laughed. "A serial killer who stalks women who are only interested in one specific obscure poet that he happens to be related to? Doubtful. Maybe you should meet him too. Or you could even come with me."

"Maybe," Julian agreed, sounding uncertain. "If you decide to go, let me know, and I'll see if I can get off work, okay?" Greta murmured her agreement. They chatted for a little while longer, then said goodnight.

Greta was on her way to the bathroom to brush her teeth when the phone rang again. She smiled to herself as she picked it up, thinking that she wouldn't mind a little 'pillow talk' with Julian before going to sleep, but when she looked at the caller ID, it was Michael.

"Hello?" she answered tentatively.

"Oh Greta, hi. I just wanted to make sure you got back to your hotel room safely."

"Yes, no problems. The cab driver dropped me off right at the front lobby."

"Good. Well, anyway...let me know if you'll be able to come to Champs Blancs as soon as you talk to your fiancé, all right?"

"I will." Greta was feeling a little pressured, so she quickly added, "Listen, I have to go—I have the shower running." They said goodbye and she hung up. Almost immediately, the phone rang again.

"Ugh," she said out loud, letting it go to voicemail. While she was brushing her teeth, she heard it ring again. She ignored it. When she came back in the room, she listened to the message. It was Helen. "Jesus Christ, Greta! Answer the fucking phone! It's an emergency!" She sounded like she was crying.

Greta was about to dial Helen's number when her ringer went off. This time she answered it. "Helen—what the hell? What's going on?"

Helen sobbed hysterically into the phone, then she screamed, "It's Mom. She's dead!"

Chapter 10: Louisa
1891

I am weary and sick in both body and soul. My life, which was once so simple and full of joy, has become a dark labyrinth. I am lost within a maze of death and decay and I have become insensible to the horrors I have both witnessed and performed.

Lucius's body was heavy and I was weak, but fear—and hatred—compelled me forward. I spent the day huddled in the parlour, for there was nowhere else to go where I would not be surrounded by death. Once the sun had set, I dragged his lifeless form from my bedchamber and down the stairs, then out into the yard where I breathed the night air deeply, contemplating my sins. I will not escape damnation, this I know. There will be no salvation for either of us, and Lucius will be awaiting me in the fiery depths of hell.

With a strength I did not know I possessed, I hauled him to the well. I pulled up the bucket, its dark depths shimmering in the moonlight, and then I hoisted Lucius onto the edge and tipped him over, a sack of flesh that was as unfamiliar to me as a stranger. There was a distant splash as he settled into his watery grave. I turned my back and carried the bucket to the house. My clothes were covered in gore and my hands were bloody—I scrubbed and scrubbed them but, like Lady Macbeth in the Scottish play, I could not wash them clean. Perhaps the stains are only in my mind, but they are real to me. I will no longer be able to use the well—the putrefaction will make the water unpotable. But there is the cistern yet, brimming with water as I had thought. That will last me until the summer's drought has set in, and then I may travel to the river...if I am still alive in the fall. I feel as though my heart might stop at any moment. My head aches with exhaustion, yet sleep eludes me.

Very early this morning, before the town would be stirring, I dressed and walked to the church. It is a long journey by foot, but I used my time well, preparing my tale for Pastor Campbell. His shock was palpable when he saw me on the doorstep of the manse. He hurried me inside immediately and had his housemaid fetch some tea. "Whatever has happened?" he asked. "You look as if you have seen a ghost."

"My father is dead," I told him flatly. I had been afraid that I was too numb to weep, but at the pronouncement of those terrible words, I was overcome with grief and sobbed for several moments as he stared at me in amazement and sympathy. I related the events to him—not, of course, the true events, but the fabricated story that I had concocted—that I had been ill and had taken to bed, and that unbeknownst to me, Father was similarly afflicted. His heart being weak, he had succumbed without my knowledge, and that Lucius, hoping to see a fortune from the estate, deliberately withheld Father's passing from me. But once he realized that we were destitute, that there was no grand inheritance, he became incensed. He fired the servants in a fury—I had no idea where they fled to—and then took the horses and abandoned me to Champs Blancs.

"Where has he gone?!" Pastor Campbell exclaimed, astounded at the callousness of my brother. If only he knew the truth—what would he think then?

"I do not know," I prevaricated, sobbing once more into my handkerchief. I cried not for Lucius but for Father. Father had once said that we were cursed, that his brain sickness, his 'turns' were common to the male line, and that he was fortunate to have found Mother, a woman whose own sweet nature tempered his. Yet nothing could prevent Lucius from inheriting not a fortune, not land and holdings, but the same madness that tormented Father.

Pastor Campbell comforted me and then took me back to Champs Blancs in his cabriolet. I demurred when he asked about stabling his horse, telling him that with the departure of Beechcroft, I couldn't say what state the stables were in. I am sickened by how easily I could lie to this good man of God, but he believed me and left the cabriolet and Samson, his horse, in the drive. Then I led him into the house and up the stairs to Father's chambers.

Poor Pastor Campbell. Nothing could have prepared him for the sight of Father, fetid and rotting in his bed. He said a prayer—said more than one—and then took me to the parlour to discuss what we should do next.

"You will come to the manse and stay there until the undertaker has finished. I will send my housekeeper to set the room to rights."

"No," I protested. "I need to stay at Champs Blancs. I feel Father's spirit here so strongly, and I must commune with him. He will be interred on the grounds next to Mother, of course. He loved her so, and it is only proper that they be reunited for eternity. Perhaps she will also make her presence known after all this time." Pastor Campbell looked at me with empathy. He was not unfamiliar with the prevailing practice of seances and such, having held more than one himself for townsfolk whose kin had passed on.

"I understand," he said, but insisted on returning to me to see the body removed and the room refreshed. I offered him profuse thanks and he departed to the undertaker's, promising to bring back support. I sat alone, steeling myself for the moment that Father's empty shell would be carried from the house.

Saturday, May 9th

I barely slept a wink last night, having taken refuge in the parlour. I curled up in one of the easy chairs, trying unsuccessfully to calm my mind, to no avail. Pastor Campbell had returned after lunch with a crew of men from town, some bearing black crepe wreaths for the doors, and some with more practical tools. The Pastor's housekeeper arrived and she began to cover the mirrors and stop all the clocks. When she asked what time they should arrest, I was helpless and muttered, "Fifteen minutes to midnight", not knowing exactly when Father had passed. She came into the parlour some time later and announced that Mrs. Mersey had arrived, having heard the sad news of Father's passing. I declined taking her call. How could I face her, after all that had happened? It was a credit to her indeed that she saw fit to come to my aid, and while I was distraught at turning her away, it was better that she remain unsullied by my family's sins.

Then, this morning, a messenger arrived with a package. It was from Mrs. Mersey and it contained mourning clothes. The note within was written in her kind hand: "My dearest Louisa. Please forgive me but I have taken the liberty of going to the dressmaker's. They have used the dimensions for your ball gown to find an appropriate costume for you, that you may mourn properly. Please accept this gift and know that our thoughts— mine, Mr. Mersey's, and Tomas's—are with you at this sad time."

I buried my face in the garment and sobbed silently for a life that might have been, imagining myself not in funereal garb but in wedding clothes, with Father standing proudly by as Tomas made me his wife, the Merseys looking on joyously. All but for Lucius...I cannot forgive him, nor can I forgive myself.

Sunday, May 10ᵗʰ

The funeral for Father will take place on Tuesday. I have eschewed a wake—he was cold in his bed for long enough to ensure that he was truly deceased. Pastor Campbell had his man bring back the coffin to rest in the formal living room, leaving me the parlour for my solitude and grief. He has agreed that on Tuesday morning, the undertakers will transport the body to the hill on the grounds of Champs Blancs where Mother was laid to rest. They will be together once again. At my insistence, there will be no mourners save Pastor Campbell and myself. We have no family nearby to pay respects, and I have no desire to become a spectacle for the people of the town.

But there is one thing that weighs on my mind. The stable. Thus far, I have managed to keep the Pastor, his staff, and the undertakers away from it with the reasoning that I found it unsuitable for habitation by their horses, and they took me at my word, although I perceived that the request seemed eccentric to them. Nevertheless, they respected my wishes, and as of yet, no one is aware of the dreadful secrets it contains. However, I cannot prevent an intrusion forever, and I am terrified that someone will discover the bodies. Already, the flies have clustered and if one stands too close to the structure, the stench is palpable—it will not be long before the vultures begin to circle. I have determined that the best course of action is to simply set it ablaze. Champs Blancs is secluded enough that it may not draw attention until it has been quite immolated, and the pyre shall serve as a tribute to those innocents within.

🦗 🦗 🦗

It is done. I carried a candle into the barn late in the afternoon. I had to cover my face with a handkerchief to avoid retching from the smell of decay and old blood. Touching the flame to the bottom layer of the hay mound, I waited a moment until it caught, then hastened from the stable and hid in the house. I could hear the roar of the inferno, but could not bring myself to watch. I cannot say for whom I felt more grief—Jack and Fancy, those two gentle souls, or Mabel and Beechcroft, who might have known happiness together, but instead are huddled beside each other in cruel death.

Tuesday, May 12th

The funeral for Father took place this morning. The undertakers had prepared the ground, and there was little left for me to do, save toss a handful of cold dirt upon the pine box he was buried in, having not the funds to provide him with something more befitting his station. Pastor Campbell was initially concerned; after seeing the remains of the stable, he queried me regarding the events that led to its destruction. I pleaded innocence, and implied that it might have been the work of mischief-makers, knowing that I was alone in the house. He agreed that it was fortunate Lucius had absconded with the horses, but desired that I call for the local constable regarding the fire. I reassured him that I would do so; however, I have no intention of drawing any further attention to Champs Blancs. And as for this volume of my thoughts and feelings—I shall put it away until such time as I need to record something more hopeful than grief and loss.

Friday, June 5th

Reading back my last entry, I almost laugh when I think of the optimism contained in those last lines, for now I write once more with unthinkable news. My monthly courses have still not come, and I fear the worst. I have no one to turn to and cannot bear the thought of the humiliation I will suffer—and the questions that will inevitably arise. Suspicion will surely fall upon Tomas Mersey if my situation becomes known, and he will become the centre of the town's gossip, the scandal preventing him from finding the happiness that I will never possess. I have written to a distant cousin outside of Montreal, hoping an offer might be made to take me in for a time as I grieve the loss of Father. I did not disclose the true reason for my request, nor did I mention Lucius. I have decided that if no refuge is forthcoming, I will seek the same fate as Lucius, but by my own hand. I am already sentenced to hell, with no chance for redemption, and I would rather suffer the torments of eternal damnation than live as an outcast, and force the same fate on an innocent child.

Tuesday, June 30th

I have spent these last almost three weeks pacing the halls of Champs Blancs like a madwoman, stricken with fear for both myself and the unborn child, whom I now have no doubt about. Thankfully, the response came three days ago that Mr. Sebastien Duberger, my cousin, and his wife, Sophie, would be pleased to host me for an extended visit. I leave tomorrow. I have closed up the house, packed what little I own, and prepared a convincing story to explain my condition. Pastor Campbell has kindly agreed to take me to the train station in Wolverton. I am desolated at leaving Champs Blancs behind. I carry this volume with me and will record the events to come, whatever that shall be, for posterity when I arrive, hoping only that you, the reader of the future, will not judge me as harshly as I judge myself. I leave you with this until we meet again:

> *A hundred days are one dark night*
> *And all is black that once was white.*
> *For those of us without an aim*
> *Where life or death seem all the same.*

Part Two

Requiem
1891

To The One Who Chains My Soul:

I starve, I dream, I wake, I starve again. You will not be mine, no matter how I beg. Oh L., you tear my heart to pieces and I watch the life's blood pour from my empty shell while you watch, hard and cold, aware of my suffering yet refusing to ease it. But what prevents you? A god who tells you it is wrong, immoral? Cast that god aside and worship before the altar of the shrine I erect to you and only you. Let us live as we always have done—sequestered, cloistered, known only to one another. We are the same in soul and mind—let not the archaic teachings of a repressive society allow you to throw away the happiness you know we have together. There is nothing left to prevent us from living as wife and husband, just as the Greek gods and ancient Egyptians once did. And Eve herself came from Adam's rib—even they shared blood and bone. Let us enjoy the paradise that was built for us, with no serpent to taint our more than sibling love. Alas, I fear you will once again meet my pleas with disgust, and can only hope time will change your mind.

The One Who Lives in Torment

Chapter 11: Greta

The funeral for Greta's mother had been appropriately gloomy, and the mourners, few that there were, stood huddled under black umbrellas as a cold downpour descended from the heavens onto them, splashing the upturned piles of dirt with heavy drops, creating pools of mud around the open hole in the cemetery ground and the casket above it. The officiant spoke briefly, some canned little speech about God's love. She hadn't known Tammy, or any of the family, but had been provided by the funeral home as part of the basic package that Greta was able to afford. Afterwards, Greta and Julian took refuge under a willow tree, its fronds dripping with rain, waiting for Helen. She had stood next to the casket, sobbing relentlessly, almost luxuriously, making a spectacle of herself in front of the funeral director and his staff, the only other attendees aside from a strange woman who claimed to have known Tammy. Greta wondered if it was the same woman who'd been with her mother outside the train station. Regardless, she assumed that they had been using together before Tammy had died of an overdose. Meth laced with fentanyl, the police had said. The woman left immediately after the graveside service, but not before asking Greta if she had any money to spare. Greta took in the woman's skeletal frame, rotting teeth, and scarred arms, and was about to demur quietly, saying that neither she nor Julian carried cash, when she remembered Tammy, and the guilt she still felt about the last time she'd seen her. She pulled out a twenty-dollar bill—the woman gave her a grateful look and then hurried away without a backwards glance.

"Helen!" Greta finally called out. "If you want to ride back with us, we're leaving in a minute!" Helen didn't respond.

"Where exactly are we taking her?" Julian asked quietly. "Does she have a place to stay? Or are you going to let her bunk with you indefinitely?"

Greta sighed. "I have no idea. Having Helen in my space is the last thing I want, but I can hardly kick her out onto the street now that Tammy's dead." Greta had stopped referring to her mother in any way other than by her first name years ago, after the third time she and Helen had been dropped at their grandparents' house with no idea when their mother would return. Greta had been fifteen at the time, and decided that Tammy didn't deserve an affectionate moniker. Helen had only been ten, and took the abandonment much harder. When Tammy had reached out years later, Greta wanted nothing to do with her, having come to view her maternal grandmother as the mother figure Tammy had never been, while Helen, eager to reconnect, had done it in the worst way. Greta was internally furious with Helen—surely she knew that Tammy was back on the pipe, and not only did she *not* say anything, she probably encouraged it, maybe even smoked with her. It was only sheer luck that Helen hadn't been there when Tammy took her fatal last hit.

"If she doesn't have anywhere else to go, I'll give her a couple of days to get back on her feet," she told Julian, then yelled again. "Helen!"

Her sister turned, wiping her running nose with her hand. "All *right!*" she responded angrily, stomping over to the willow tree. "Can you believe that bitch?" she grumbled. "Mom would have hated all that 'God' stuff." She stood, sniffling, waiting.

"Okay, well, I guess we better go. If you're ready. So where do you want us to drop you off?" Julian asked, trying to sound casual.

Helen looked at both of them with astonishment. "Dropped off? Are you fucking kidding? Where the hell am I supposed to go, *Greta*? You know Arion kicked me out. Nice way to treat your sister after the only person who genuinely cared about her DIED!" She started sobbing again, turning her back on both Greta and Julian, who looked at each other. Greta felt helpless and gestured silently at Helen; Julian rolled his eyes.

"No, Helen, it's all right. You can come back to my place and stay with me until you figure out what you're going to do." Greta knew she was going to regret it, but how could she let Helen fend for herself on the streets after what had just happened to Tammy? Helen stomped back over without a word, as if *she* was the one doing Greta and Julian the favour.

They all got into Julian's car and arrived at the house Greta shared, barely a few words uttered between them. Helen got out without thanking Julian and went inside right away. Greta stayed behind for a moment. "I'm so sorry," she started. "I know that this is—"

"This is what?" Julian interrupted, taking her hand. "You, trying to do the best you can for your sister? Honestly, Greta, don't worry about me. I just want to make sure that you're okay. I know you and your mother weren't close, and that your sister is a...an addict, so if there's anything at all I can do, just let me know. Like, if you want me to drive her to the outskirts of town and leave her there, I'm your guy."

Greta laughed and her eyes welled up with tears. "You're too good to me, you know that? I only hope my roommates are as understanding about still having Helen living with me—it's a small enough house as it is without adding an extra person. You and I need to get an apartment together soon—then I'll have a proper excuse as to why she has to find her own place. I just wish I had the money to rent her a room somewhere. After the funeral costs, I don't have any cash to spare but I really need to get her out of my hair before I go to Champs Blancs."

Julian's brow furrowed. "You're still planning to take that guy up on his offer?"

"Well, yeah. I thought you were okay with it. I have to keep going with my research—and he might be the only one who can help me. But if you really don't want me to go..."

"No, it's fine. I mean, I'll meet him when I drop you off, right? And if I get a weird vibe, you're coming back with me, no questions asked." Michael had offered once again to pick Greta up, but Julian insisted on taking her so that he could ensure she was safely delivered to Michael Shepherd's home—and that way, he could vet the man for himself.

"I wish I could stay with you," he said. "It would be great to have a couple of days away, just the two of us—aside from your research pal being in the other part of the house, anyway."

Michael, when Greta had emailed him to say that her mother had suddenly passed away and that she wouldn't be able to take him up on his invitation for a couple of weeks, had responded that he had decided to turn part of the house into a country inn, so once she was ready, she could stay with him and have a whole massive wing to herself, free of charge.

"You'll be my test case," he told her, delighted. "You can let me know if there are any issues or bugs that need to be worked out. I really want this place to become a destination—I don't mean to sound like I'm trying to capitalize on Louisa, but it occurred to me that the home of a famous poet—and she *will* be famous after you publish your thesis and we do a little marketing—would be a real draw! I'm literally about to restore and redecorate what I think was her bedroom—and I'm hoping to be finished by the time you arrive, so you can say you slept in Louisa Duberger's room!"

Greta still felt a little unsure about the whole arrangement, but so far, Michael had been nothing but nice, in a normal, regular way. She'd put what she'd initially thought was controlling behaviour down to simply a man who was used to doing his own thing, and no other red flags had popped up. And when she told Dr. Weldon about the visit, he was initially hesitant, but then said, "There are so many people who will know exactly where you are—I can't see him doing you any harm. He sounds, as you say, lonely, and looking to make a stronger connection with his family through your help. It could be quite exciting—who knows what else lurks within those attic walls? Maybe once he has the guest wing properly set up, I'll book a couple of nights myself!"

Greta had felt better having talked to her professor and reassured Julian that Dr. Weldon was right. "Michael would be suspect number one if anything happened to me—I doubt he wants any negative publicity if he's trying to start a successful business."

She and Julian sat in the car for a few minutes more, then she reluctantly got out. "Time to have a conversation with Helen," she said. "Help her plan out her future. Wish me luck."

Julian gave her a thumbs up and drove away. He'd offered to stay for moral support, but Greta knew that would make Helen instantly defensive, as if they were ganging up on her. She hung her jacket in the closet and went into the kitchen, where Helen was staring into the refrigerator. As she reached for a container of leftover chicken and rice, Greta stopped her. "That's not ours. You can't take it."

Helen sighed and put the container back, muttering under her breath, "Such a goody two shoes."

"Forget the food for a minute. We need to talk." Greta sat down at the kitchen table and gestured to one of the chairs.

Helen groaned and shuffled over, dropping herself hard into the chair and crossing her arms across her chest, already defiant, defensive. "Here it comes," she said, looking at the ceiling, refusing to meet Greta's eyes. "What? You want me gone, right? Fine. Tell me where to go and how to pay for it, and I'll pack up right now."

Greta inhaled sharply. "Helen, you can't just crash on the floor of my room forever. And I'll be moving in soon with Julian anyway, and then you'll *have* to find your own place."

Helen stood up, furious. "You know, Mom would never have put me out on the street. If she hadn't died—"

"I'm not your mother," Greta interrupted harshly, "and she was the reason you were on the streets in the first place, so don't give me that manipulative bullshit. Here's the deal. You have two weeks to find a job and get a place of your own, even if it's some cheap hotel room until you start getting paid. I'll front you the first few days, and then it's up to you. I'm leaving for Champs Blancs next Monday so you can stay here until I'm back—and then you need to go."

"Seriously?! Fine!" Helen yelled, grabbing her coat. "I'll *go*— back to Arion and start selling for him like he wanted. I hope you're happy!"

"Jesus, Helen," Greta rolled her eyes. "You have an opportunity here, to get a real job and live a good life away from all that. You're an adult—start acting like one! Or do you want to end up like Tammy, dead in some fleabag motel?!"

"At least she loved me." Helen's eyes welled up with tears. She slung her bag over her shoulder, went out the door, and disappeared into the night. Greta felt sick. There was nothing she could do for Helen, at least not now. When their grandparents had passed away, Grandma not long after Grandpa, she and Helen had received a small inheritance. Helen had squandered hers on drugs and alcohol, for both her and Tammy, while Greta had put hers into savings, using most of it to help fund her education and living expenses. But now that was gone, and paying for a hotel room would put her into debt. She hoped once she was back from Champs Blancs and the new term started, that the research assistant job that Dr. Weldon had promised would materialize. Either that, or she'd have to work at the antique market just to get by. Julian was always suggesting it—maybe she'd be forced to take him up on it. She read for a while, reacquainting herself with Louisa Duberger's early work, hoping the sly and humorous tone of one of her favourite pieces, 'Entranced' would pull her out of the doldrums:

I chanced to meet one morning,

An aged man, so wise.

His clothes, they were of ancient cut,

And shifty were his eyes.

He spoke to me in tones so low,

Of marvels he had seen.

Places travelled, mystic names,

Where I had never been.

So intent, I sat transfixed,

For hours the old sage spoke.

It was as if my own desires,

Had suddenly awoke.

At length I had to break away,

Though still his stories flowed.

We parted in our separate ways,

To each his homebound road.

But reaching home, I came to earth,

I laughed though twasn't funny.

For as the elder stole my thoughts,

He also stole my money.

She laughed right along with Louisa, always delighted by the twist at the end. An appropriate warning for others, she thought, as it occurred to her that she should probably hide her wallet somewhere; Helen would have no problem stealing one of her credit cards if she had the chance. She was tempted to call Julian—she was sure he was dying to know how her conversation with Helen had gone, but she was too exhausted to rehash the whole thing.

She finally went to bed, still no sign of Helen, and left the front door open just in case. Her roommates had locks on their own doors, and they were all in for the night, so it wouldn't be a problem. She stayed awake for a while, lying in bed, thinking and waiting, then gave up and fell soundly asleep. When she woke in the morning, Helen was lying facedown across the blow-up mattress that Greta had borrowed from one of her roommates.

She was still wearing the clothes she'd had on for the funeral, but she looked dishevelled, her arms and legs askew. Greta's stomach clenched; she sat up in bed and watched for a few minutes to make sure Helen was breathing.

As she stared at her sister, Greta came to a realization. She couldn't do it anymore. She couldn't deal with Helen and her drama, the stress and anxiety, the overwhelming guilt, the constant worry that she'd get a call, not unlike the one she'd just gotten about Tammy, telling her that her sister was finally dead, or worse, murdered by some dealer or pimp. She loved Helen— or at least the Helen she'd taught to tie her shoes, helped with her homework, tried to be a better role model to her than their mother—but it was no good. The sweet, happy little girl that Helen had once been disappeared a long time ago, and Greta had nothing left for her sister. She wiped a tear from her cheek and quietly went downstairs. She called Michael Shepherd and let him know she was arriving the next day.

Chapter 12: Louisa
1891

Wednesday, July 15th

I have arrived at Maison de Lierre, the home of my cousin Sebastien and his wife, after an arduous journey. The train was noisy and it took the better part of two days to complete the trip, with numerous stops along the way. My corset had begun to bind terribly and I was racked by nausea the entire time, unable to eat more than a few mouthfuls of the light supper I had prepared for my travels. Fortunately, I was able to purchase cups of tea from the dinner car and they sustained me. I can only imagine what the other passengers must have thought—a young woman traveling without a companion. Several attempted to strike up conversation with me, but I refrained from socializing, preferring to sit alone staring out the window. If they only knew my circumstances, they would have shunned me instead. But I presented an unfriendly façade and eventually, I was left to myself, and to my own dreadful thoughts. With my limited funds, I was relegated to the crowded coach section, and barely slept a wink sitting upright in the hard leather seat. Whenever my eyes did close, however, I was plagued by terrible visions, of Lucius lying on the floor in a pool of blood, of Mabel and Beechcroft dead in the barn, and oh, the poor horses—but I think the worst was the image of Father, putrefying in his own bed, no one to ease his suffering as his soul passed from this life into the next. No, better not to sleep at all.

I arrived at the train station in Montreal, a bustling, modern building unlike anything I'd ever seen. I was met there by Sebastien, my elder cousin by ten years, and we travelled in his barouche to Maison de Lierre, which lies in the countryside at the edge of the city. He immediately expressed sympathy for the loss of Father, but stated that he had had no contact with that branch of the family since the time he was a boy, and that my mother, whose family was originally from England, encouraged Father to move to Ontario. He regretted that he had not been able to see Oncle Laurent in all the years before his passing, but had a vague recollection of him as a kind man. Father *was* kind, and I did not mention the occasional turns that cursed his mind, not wanting to sully his memory. Sebastien seemed pleased that I would make a visit to Maison de Lierre, even after such a tragic set of events, and was sorry that we had not been able to become acquainted sooner, under happier circumstances. His English is limited and my French is not much better, but we were able to communicate well enough. Still, it was a relief when we arrived at the house and I discovered that Sebastien's wife, Sophie, speaks English rather fluently.

She is a gentle and softspoken woman, equal in age to Sebastien, and she fussed about me like an older sister, genuinely concerned for my welfare. "You are so pale—the trip must have been very wearing upon you. We will take tea, and then you must lie down and rest. I know the train lacks the comfort of a proper bed." The house is bright and cheerful, and we enjoyed our tea in a parlour with large windows that allow the sun's rays to pour through, warming my chilled bones. I am unsure how Sebastien earned his fortune, and it would be uncouth to ask, but the barouche, the style and size of the Maison, and the number of servants I have seen thus far tell me that they are well-to-do.

After tea, Sophie led me to the bedchamber she had prepared for me, a substantial suite decorated in the latest Aesthetic style, which I was familiar with only because Mrs. Mersey had spoken of it extensively after having attended a lecture by Mr. Oscar Wilde on the subject. I had much longed to see it put into practice in person and was not disappointed. Sophie's brow creased with concern when I stood, staring up at the intricately painted ceiling, mistaking my silence for displeasure. "Is it not to your liking?" she asked, her French accent most charming. "I can have something larger prepared for you."

"Oh, no!" I hastened to reassure her. "It is truly delightful. I shall be most comfortable here, do not fear." She left me to unpack my small valise, advising me that dinner would be at 8 pm and that the housemaid would wake me in time to dress.

Once she was gone, I sank onto the bed in despair. I felt such a fraud, a charlatan. They were generous and kind people, and I was a stain upon their household. How could I continue to hold my head up high and smile, and behave as if nothing was wrong? It was almost too much to bear. Then I thought of the child growing within me, innocent and pure. This might be my only chance to secure a future for the infant, and for myself. Exhausted, I fell into a deep sleep, and knew nothing until there was a loud rapping at my door. I stumbled, disoriented, to answer the knock, and opened the door to behold a young woman, younger than I, wearing a uniform and smiling.

"Mistress has asked me to tell you that dinner will be served shortly. Do you need assistance in dressing or refreshing your hair?" She spoke in French but I understood her well enough by her gestures.

As much as I would have adored her attentions, I could feel the nausea that had afflicted me on the train rising again. "Non, merci," I attempted to smile in return and answered in my own limited French. "I can manage. But thank you for the offer."

She curtsied slightly, and excused herself. I sat back down on the bed for a moment, breathing deeply until I felt slightly better. Once I had calmed my stomach, I went to the large wooden wardrobe with gilt handles where I had hung my one good dress—or at least the one which still fit me. Although the material had been fairly expensive, it was an old gown, shabby in comparison to the stylish day dress that my hostess wore earlier. And while I abhorred the thought of their pity, I felt sure that both Sophie and my cousin would refrain from negative commentary. I remembered the beautiful silk gown that I had worn on the fateful night of the Spring Ball, and wished that I had something similar to don. Thinking about the ball did nothing but increase my anxiety—Lucius and Tomas Mersey in a public conflict while I stood alone, an object of derision, made so by my brother's behaviour...I realized that I had wasted some minutes on an unwanted reverie and finished dressing in haste.

True to my speculation, I was received with compliments on my choice of evening wear, and the meal commenced soon after. I was still feeling nauseated, and more was the pity, for the repast was excellent and obviously designed to tempt me. I ate what I could, claiming fatigue as an excuse, although I did indulge in a slice of delicious Battenburg cake.

Once the meal was finished, we all enjoyed a small glass of brandy, then Sebastien removed himself to his study, while Sophie and I retired to the parlour. A fire had been lit, creating a warm and soothing atmosphere, and we sat in down-filled armchairs on either side of the hearth. Finally, Sophie spoke, with some hesitation. "Please accept my condolences on the loss of your dear father," she began. I murmured my thanks and she continued. "I don't mean to intrude but...I was under the impression from Sebastien that you had an older brother?"

"Yes," I replied quietly, already considering the direction this conversation might take, and preparing my narrative.

"But where is he? Surely he cannot have left you to suffer alone, yet you made no mention of him in your letter." She reached over and touched my hand in a gesture of sympathy.

I placed my other hand on top of hers and breathed in deeply. "I can hardly bear to admit it," I said, raising my eyes to hers. "When he discovered that Father's fortune was not what he believed it to be, he abandoned me, claiming that he could not live a pauper. He absconded with the horses, leaving me with naught. It..." and here I lowered my eyes once more, "it broke my heart."

Sophie gasped in disbelief and squeezed my hand more tightly. "You may not fear," she said. "You are family, and we will endeavour to ensure that you are provided for. Indeed, I already feel a sisterhood with you, and will do my best to support you...in any way you might need."

Her turn of phrase caught me off-guard. Could she have guessed at least one part of my secret? I went to my chambers soon after, pondering her meaning and fearing the worst.

Friday, July 17th

It was as I had conjectured—Sophie has found me out. Yesterday was a quiet day. I was left to myself to acclimatize to Maison de Lierre. I spent the morning wandering the house and grounds, admiring the grand ballroom, the large dining room with its wainscotting and gas-lit chandelier, and mentally cataloguing the flowers in their sprawling gardens. In the afternoon, I attempted to write, but little inspiration came to me. Not only have I lost everything that I had hoped for, even my imagination fails me now. Later, I took tea alone with Sophie, Sebastien having driven to town to oversee the expansion of his textile factory, the existence of which explains their good fortune and the size of the house. Sophie was quiet and lost in thought for most of the time we were in each other's company, and I thought nothing of it until today.

I took breakfast in my room in order to avoid anyone witnessing me purge my stomach after the meal. I cannot keep anything down it seems, and it would be best for no one to see me so indisposed. As well, I am finding that the wearing of a corset is torture in itself and the longer I can avoid it, the better. I finally descended mid-morning and found Sophie in the parlour, a pair of knitting needles in hand. When she looked up and saw me, she smiled and put the wool and needles back into the tapestry basket by her chair.

"Have you slept well, my dear?" she inquired, settling her hands in her lap.

"Yes. The bed is most comfortable, thank you," I responded. She continued to stare at me until I felt quite nervous.

"Louisa," she began. "You may consider me as a sister, may you not?" I nodded, anxious to know what had prompted this entry into conversation. She drew a deep breath. "And if we are indeed sisters, you may be completely open and honest with me, may you not?"

A sense of dread came over me. I nodded once more, fear trapping my tongue.

"Then let me ask you boldly and let you answer candidly, between only you and me, as sisters. I have noticed that you eat little, and the maid tells me you are sick in the morning. Your clothes seem ill-fitting and you strain against your corset—no, let me finish," she admonished gently as I protested. "You see that Sebastien and I are childless. Yet I am no stranger to that blessing, and I have had the joy of motherhood in my heart three times. It is my life's tragedy that I cannot carry a pregnancy for any longer than a month or two." At this, her eyes filled with tears. "I know the signs, dear sister." She paused and wiped away a tear. "Are you...with child? I beg you, tell me truthfully."

I hung my head in shame. How could I continue to prevaricate when I was so transparent to her? And if I told her the truth, would it lead to my salvation as I had hoped? "I can hardly stand to admit it," I whispered, "but yes."

"Oh, my poor dear." She put her fingers gently beneath my chin and lifted my face to meet hers. "All will be well."

Chapter 13: Greta

Julian pulled up in front of Greta's house right after lunch. It was a gorgeous afternoon, and Greta breathed in the scent of roses as she carried her bag down the walkway to the car, grateful that Mr. Selensky had allowed her to plant the bushes a couple of years ago. "It's your money," he said. "Hope you have a green thumb." She didn't know whether she did or not, but she had done a lot of research on the care of roses, and now the bushes had grown large, bursting with fragrant buds.

"Thanks for doing this on such short notice," she said, as she threw her bag in the back of the car then settled into the passenger seat. "I really couldn't take any more of Helen clomping around, refusing to speak to me, and talking loudly on the phone to her 'boyfriend.' I know she's trying to make me feel bad—she told him that she'd be coming back to him soon because her sister was 'kicking her out.' I reminded her that I was giving her time to find her own place, even willing to pay until she got on her feet, but no—that's not good enough. I don't know how she became so entitled. I—" She stopped and looked at Julian, who was staring straight ahead at the road and nodding mechanically.

"I'm sorry. You're probably sick of hearing about it."

"No," he answered. "I just don't know how to help you, and it's frustrating. I'm an only child, so I've never had to go through something like this."

"I might as well be an only child myself," Greta said sadly. "I don't think Helen gives a crap about me—just what she can *get* from me. But I'm over it. Luckily, Michael had no problem with me coming earlier than we'd planned. In fact, he seemed really excited."

"I bet." Julian sounded cynical and Greta chuckled softly.

"Oh, come on," she chided him. "You two will become best bros in no time, I'm sure of it."

Julian snorted, but gave her a quick grin, then went back to watching the road. Greta looked at him in profile, again admiring his strong jaw and carved cheekbones. His eyes were large and dark brown, like chocolate, and she envied the long thick lashes that framed them. How wonderful it would be to wake up every morning to those eyes, she thought, then said aloud, "While I'm gone, promise to check out that apartment, the one I sent you the link to? I think it would be really perfect for us. Don't forget, I already gave Selensky notice, so I absolutely have to be out by the end of the month, and this place is available on June 15th."

Julian sighed. "I promise."

Greta was perplexed. "What's wrong? Why do you sound so... disinterested? Do you want to spend our marriage with you still living at your parents? Come on! We need to get a place and this one has everything—it's close to work for you, on the bus route to the university for me...they even allow pets, so we could get a dog or a cat or something, and it has a really big balcony too."

"And it's also really expensive, Greta. You should just come and live at my parents with me."

"No way!" she exclaimed. "I told you—I'll be getting a research assistant position in the fall if Dr. Weldon gets his funding, and you've been saving. Stop procrastinating—it'll be fine. Although I *will* need to stay at your parents for a little while if Helen's still around when I get back from Champs Blancs."

"Yeah, they said it was no problem. And yes, I promise to look at the apartment." He took her hand and squeezed it. "Anyway, we'll be there soon. Can you put your GPS on so we don't miss the turn?"

About twenty minutes later, the automated voice told them to go right. There didn't seem to be a road, but Greta pointed at a faded sign, almost hidden by tall weeds. Most of the paint had worn off, but they could just barely make out the words 'Champs Blancs.' They turned into an overgrown laneway beyond the sign and followed it for a minute, watching the valley up ahead get closer. Finally, they reached a point where the laneway dropped down and they could look out over the landscape in front of them. Greta gasped. "My god, is that the house?!"

Julian put the car into 'Park' then nodded silently, taking it all in. "I've never seen anything like it before." They sat for a moment, staring at the mansion below them in the valley. It was massive, a dark brick 3-story structure with a central tower flanked by two large wings, each with their own spires, gables, and numerous chimneys. The windows looked, from where Julian and Greta were observing, to be all leaded glass with carved frames. The laneway descended into the valley, coming to an end at a circular driveway in front of the house.

"How does no one know about this place?" she asked, astounded. "It's like a castle, definitely bigger than Kilbride or Annandale House. Although not as well taken care of," she added, noting the missing slate tiles on parts of the roof, and the knee-high weeds that graced the driveway below. "But still, I'm sure people would love to tour it."

"I bet someone could sneak in and live there for weeks, and the owner would never know it!" Julian speculated.

Greta shivered. "Ugh. Now that's something out of a horror movie. I hope not—at least not while I'm here!"

"Horror movie—that's not a bad idea. Michael would be better off forgetting about some kind of bed and breakfast deal and rent this place out to film companies, or murder mystery parties. People would pay a fortune for something like this. I'm so happy I took time off work to bring you—I can't wait to see inside."

He put the car back into 'Drive' and they descended into the valley. As they came closer to the house, they passed the stone foundation of an old barn, barely visible through the tall weeds, and an ancient wellhead that was covered with wooden boards. Finally, they stopped at the base of a set of sweeping carved steps that led to a huge front door. They both got out, and Greta paused for a moment, shielding her eyes with her hand and staring up at Champs Blancs. It was almost too much to believe, that this was the home of Louisa Duberger, the place where she had grown up and written such beautiful—and dark—poetry. "Maybe that's the solution to the mystery," she said, more to herself than to Julian, but he overheard her.

"What do you mean?"

"Well, I can't imagine writing anything cheerful while living in this place. Maybe her youthful work was overshadowed by the reality of Champs Blancs. It feels almost...oppressive."

Julian was about to respond when the front door flew open. Michael Shepherd strode out and stood on the top step, smiling. "I hope you didn't try ringing the doorbell," he said. "Like many things in this place, it's broken."

Greta greeted Michael and introduced Julian, who stepped forward. They shook hands and Michael said, "I've heard a lot about you."

Julian laughed. "All good, I hope. And Greta's told me a lot about you, this house, and the mysterious poet you both love so much." He reached for Greta's bag but Michael grabbed it first.

"Allow me," he said, carrying it up the stairs. He paused at the top and looked over his shoulder. "Are you coming?" He disappeared through the door.

Julian arched his eyebrows at Greta, who shrugged. "I told you he was a little...eccentric," she said quietly.

They climbed the stairs together and stepped through the door into an immense grand foyer. The floor was solid oak with intricate inlaid marquetry, and although it was badly worn and scuffed in spots, the design was still visible. The walls soared up two stories, encompassing a central staircase with upper balconies that overlooked the foyer below. The wallpaper was peeling from the walls and some of the spindles on the stair rails were broken, yet despite the grime and decay, it was an imposing interior. Michael put Greta's bag down and regarded them as they stared up at the stunning carved plaster and painted floral bouquets high above them. "It needs a lot of work, I know, but consider the potential. I've already started with the basics—kitchen and bathrooms. The plumbing hadn't been updated for decades; in fact, most of the fittings were original to the time that indoor plumbing was first installed here, probably in the 20s. Luckily, I know my way around a pipe."

Greta looked at him in amazement. "You're doing all the upgrades yourself?"

"Yes, and the electrical too. It's incredible what you can learn from watching videos online. Luckily, the nearest town isn't too far by car, and the local library doesn't mind me setting up shop for a while and enjoying their internet."

"So you don't have wifi here?" Julian asked.

"No, sorry, and no cell service either. We're too far from the main road to get hooked up, and down in this valley so deep that wireless service is a near impossibility. Like I said, when I need to use the internet or make a call, I go into town for a little while. There's also a nice café with free wifi where you can get the best pie—any kind you want."

Julian checked his phone skeptically, but Michael was right— no bars. He looked concerned but said nothing. Michael waited a moment, then asked, "Are you up for a quick tour before you have to go?"

Julian nodded enthusiastically and Greta took his hand, as

Michael led them up the stairs. At the top, they paused at the balcony railing, Michael explaining his plans to refinish the foyer floors. "Definitely a lot of work, but I've already rented a power sander. It'll be worth it to bring back the lustre to that oak."

Greta looked down at the floor far below, imagining it looking pristine. "I can't believe there's no local heritage society interested in helping you restore the house. You'd think they'd be thrilled to have a piece of history like this in their own back yard."

"The old couple who lived here kept to themselves for years and the house isn't visible from the main road, so not a lot of people know it exists. But even if they did, who's interested in centuries-old mansions these days? Too much upkeep and expense. No, all the kids today want is cheap little condo apartments with pools and gyms," Michael grumbled. He didn't notice the look that Greta and Julian gave each other, and Greta certainly had no intention of admitting that was exactly what she and Julian wanted. Or at least what *she* wanted.

They continued the tour, visiting first the wing where Michael was currently living, and then the wing on the other side of the house where Greta would be staying, leaving her bag on the large canopy bed to be unpacked later. Michael had done some decorating and painting in the guest quarters and while it wasn't completely finished, it was still brighter and less shabby than the rest of the house.

"It's spectacular!" she exclaimed, wandering around and staring out the floor-to-ceiling windows at the fields beyond the house. "And you think this was Louisa's room?"

"Maybe," Michael responded, shrugging, but then quickly changed the subject. "The redecorating was easy—I basically copied the style of a historic home near Lake Erie. The only hard part was the floor—it was badly stained with something that had seeped right into the grain. Fortunately, the wood's very thick—it took a lot of power sanding to make it less noticeable." He gestured at a faint area next to the bed where the pigment was slightly darker than the rest of the wood. "I'll probably throw a rug over it eventually," he said. "Something about it bothers me."

One of the bedrooms down the hall from Greta's room had been converted into a spacious bathroom, with a large walk-in shower and separate soaking tub. She oohed at the sight of it, imagining herself luxuriating in the bath instead of grabbing a quick shower before the water ran out at home.

"You like it?" Michael asked, his blue eyes bright, watching her reaction.

"Absolutely," Greta responded. "It's all so fancy—like a real hotel suite." She pointed to a tray on the counter by the sink that held miniature containers of shampoo, conditioner, and body lotion, as well as several bottles of water.

"I've tried," Michael said proudly. "By the way, the bottled water is there for you to use. Don't drink the tap water. It comes from an old well, and it's not safe. There's a cistern for cooking and so on, which isn't very convenient and it's dependent upon the rain. I'm planning to have a new well dug and install a filtration system, but for now…"

"Thanks for the warning," she said, taking one last look as they left the impressive bathroom. "I think any guests you have in the future are going to love what you've done. And if the rest of the house ends up as stunning as this part, you'll be making money hand over fist as an inn owner."

Michael laughed and ran his fingers through his graying hair. "Oh, I hope so. This is a huge—and expensive—undertaking, especially now that I'm...retired. But it's just so good to be home."

Julian interjected. "Retired? That's great. So what was it that you did exactly—I mean, before you started restoring 'centuries-old mansions'? If you don't mind me asking."

"Not at all," Michael answered expansively, putting his hands in his pockets. "I was in software. Started my own tech company a while back, then sold it to one of the larger corporations for a very tidy profit. Now I just dabble in a variety of things...restoration, research, and a little human resources, let's say."

Julian nodded, seemingly satisfied, and they finished their tour back where they started, in the main foyer. They stood, all staring at each other for a minute, then Julian cleared his throat. "I suppose I should get back," he said reluctantly. "But if there's no cell service here, how can I reach you?"

"Good question." Greta turned to Michael for suggestions.

"We can always drive into town later...or tomorrow, if we get busy. I'm sure you two lovebirds don't have to talk every night, do you?"

Greta smiled and shook her head, feeling slightly uncomfortable, and took Julian's hand. "I'll walk you to the car."

"I'll be in the kitchen," Michael told her, pointing. "Just through that door next to the stairs."

Once they were outside, and out of Michael's earshot, Greta faced Julian. "Well?"

"I don't know. He's weird, for sure, but seems harmless enough. And there's a lock on your bedroom door. Plus, he knows that I know you're here, and I'm twice as big as him, so if I don't hear from you by tomorrow night, this lovebird is going to come back and kick the door down."

Greta snickered. "Lovebirds. He must have seen you making 'googly eyes' at me."

"Neither of those things is something anyone says anymore," Julian scoffed. "He's too young to be that old-fashioned. Like I said, weird. Anyway, I'd better get going, leave you to your adventures. If I go straight back, I can make it to work on time to help with closing. Call me tonight, or if you can't, by the end of the day tomorrow at least or—" he continued in a Terminator voice, "I'll be back."

They kissed goodbye, and Greta waved as he drove off. She had a fleeting impulse to run down the laneway after him, but then he disappeared from sight over the top of the hill. Sighing, she went back into the house. It seemed darker, less friendly somehow without Julian there. She found the door to the kitchen that Michael had pointed out, and followed a narrow hallway until it opened up to the kitchen. Michael was standing at the sink, staring out a small window. When he heard her footsteps, he spun around. "Fiancé finally gone? Good—are you ready to get started?"

Chapter 14: Louisa
1891

The hands on the clock pass a million times.

The sun rises, the sun sets.

The snow falls and the snow melts.

Yet I am here.

A window lets me view the world outside,

Flowers bloom, trees bear fruit,

Birds sing, they are free,

Yet I am not.

Sunday, August 2ⁿᵈ

We awoke this morning to the fourth day in a row of terrible humidity; however, the clouds are building and the rains will come soon to break the heat. We have returned from church and I removed myself to my chambers to write in order that Sophie may broach a certain topic with Sebastien. We have spoken little since the day she guessed my dilemma and I provided her with a story that seemed to satisfy her; her only comment was to say that we must carry on as normal until such time as she could conceive a plan that would solve the problem. She said nothing more on the matter until Friday, when Sebastien was at the factory in town. She took me into the parlour and shut the door. I feared the worst—had she changed her mind? Was she disgusted by my predicament? But no.

"We must be brief," she began, "in case one of the servants overhears our conversation. I have an idea that will benefit both of us, but before I can approach Sebastien, you and I must align the narrative."

I nodded, relieved beyond all hope. "What shall we say?" I asked, eyes downcast.

"Well," she mused a moment. "You say that the father was a local gentleman, and that he died not long after your father, presumably from the same illness that took dear Oncle Laurent's life, but spared you?"

"Indeed," I answered her, ashamed of my necessary duplicity. "We were to be engaged but he was taken ill. He had made me a promise in private, and I was so confident in him, and so in love, that...if he hadn't died, we would be married now, and none of this would be necessary." I allowed a tear to fall from my eye. I have found now that whenever it seems appropriate to weep, I only need conjure up an image of Father on his deathbed and the tears flow easily.

Sophie reached over and took my hand firmly. "You must be resolute. This is my proposal. Sebastien and I have longed for a child but God has not blessed us. Our doctor has told us that there is no hope. Yet here is a sign that we should be mother and father. I will tell Sebastien about your young man—what was his name?"

I stumbled a moment in my mind. What name could I say? What name *should* I say? Finally: "His name was...Tomas Mersey. But I beg you, keep this between the two of us. His family does not know of the child and might make a claim."

"Yes, of course! I will tell Sebastien that you *were* engaged, for what difference can it truly make? And that the young man died suddenly, leaving you with child, unbeknown to his family who...opposed the match. And—," she began to speak more quickly with excitement, quite caught up in the dramatic tale, "you have agreed that once the child is born, Sebastien and I will take it for our own, leaving you to return home without scandal. Does this idea please you?"

I began sobbing in earnest, so overcome was I by her generosity. Imagine, a fatherless child, a bastard created not from love but hate, able to come into this life with *two* parents who would raise him as their own. He need never fear the sting of society's rejection. And I? I could return to Champs Blancs and live out my days in the solitude I desperately craved. I finally recovered myself and asked, "But will Sebastien agree?"

"I believe he will," she assured me. "He knows how unbearably unhappy I am without a child, and having an heir would please him very much. And of course, we would provide you with a small allowance for yourself once the child was born and you have returned home."

So now I wait, anxiously anticipating Sebastien's reaction to his wife's proposal. And if he says no, and forces me out of the house? I shall have no choice but to return to Champs Blancs and face the future alone.

❀ ❀ ❀

It is done. Sebastien has agreed. Sophie told me he accepted her plan with no argument, on the condition that the child never know its true parentage. I concur as well—it would destroy a child to learn it was the product of an unholy union, that its very identity was fraud. Going forward, I am to cloister myself, appearing only to the servants, at least until I am no longer able to hide my maternity. Sophie, meanwhile, will begin to create the illusion of a swelling waist, allowing herself to be observed by the household, eventually wearing loose gowns to create a show of fullness. When the time comes, a midwife whose discretion can be wholly trusted, will deliver the child from me and present it to Sophie. No one need ever be the wiser. Finally, I can breathe.

Tuesday, August 4ᵗʰ

Now that the 'truth' is known, Sebastien and Sophie are being exceptionally thoughtful and kind. In all honesty, I find their attentions overwhelming, stifling even, as they attempt to encourage me to eat certain delicacies, mutton, nuts, bread, and fruit that they claim provide more nourishment for the child in my womb. I am still lacking an appetite but they insist, just as they insist that I retire to my room at regular intervals to rest on the pretense that I am absorbed in writing a new poetry collection. Sadly, I am still bereft of the inspiration to write more than a few lines at a time.

Sophie is a fine actress, as I have discovered, and she has taken to complaining—with a small but satisfied smile—about the tightness of her corset when her lady's maid is present, as well as sitting in a chair by the fire with her feet up on a stool. She will play the delicate rose while I stay in my room, hiding from anyone who might guess our subterfuge. Sophie says that once my condition has become obvious, I will need to remain in my chambers and she will care for me, telling everyone that I suffer from terrible headaches and cannot manage to be in company. The realization that I will be as much a prisoner here as I was at Champs Blancs had filled me with trepidation. But I console myself that my jailers are not cruel, and their intentions are for all of our own good. And even if it is a prison, upon my release date, I will be truly free.

Tuesday, September 1ˢᵗ

I have not written much at all because nothing much has occurred since my last entry. But yesterday, Sebastien announced that I must begin my confinement. Until now, I had been able to take breakfast and dinner with he and Sophie, ensuring that I made my way downstairs while the servants were occupied and that I was seated before the food was brought to the table. In this manner I have been able to conceal my condition. But Sebastien purchased the most current treatise on maternity and is firm that, according to Dr. John West, corseting too tightly while pregnant is dangerous and can impede the natural growth of the infant. This expert suggests that women wear loose clothing and, as I cannot be perceived to be with child, Sophie has purchased voluminous gowns for us both as part of her pantomime and my truth. She is the more fortunate, because she is not yet required to confine herself. Still, she is most solicitous and has visited several times today, to bring me food and tea, and to ensure that I have a supply of books to keep me occupied.

I dare not admit to her what I will disclose here. I have begun to have nightmares again. The dreams before were of events that had taken place: Lucius, his life's blood flowing from his crushed skull, Mabel, her throat blackened with bruises, and Beechcroft, stilled by the farrier's knife. But now, these visions have become more intense. Father stalks the halls of Champs Blancs, searching for me, his nightdress torn and his skin peeling. Mabel reaches out to me beseechingly, begging me to save her. Beechcroft smiles from the horse stall right before the dagger is plunged into his chest. And Lucius? He weeps and begs my forgiveness even as I bring the candlestick down upon his head. I pray that these terrible visions do not affect the child. My emotions are so overwrought that I worry some harm may come to it. Sophie is so joyous at the thought of motherhood that it would crush her if I were to miscarry.

*Monday September 21*st

The nightmares have grown worse, leaving me exhausted and worn out. Sophie is beside herself, and paces the floor of my room, her billowing gown flowing around her, disguising *her* secret.

"You must sleep, Louisa!" she begged. "I have asked my doctor for an elixir that will help. He believes it is for me and he swears it will not harm the child—in fact, the same type of syrup is used on infants to soothe their colic. And please, I beg of you, eat some of this. Chef has prepared it specially for you." She passed me a bowl of warm oatmeal with butter and brown sugar. The smell made me nauseated but I attempted a spoonful to appease her. "My dearest," she continued, "the shadows under your eyes worry me so much. What can I do to ease your suffering?"

There was nothing to say. I could not confess my sins to her. I simply thanked her for the food and tried to choke it down as best I could with her watching. Her concern is genuine and I have agreed to try the elixir. I hope, as promised, that the child will be unharmed. As much as I hate Lucius for what he did to me, I cannot bear to disappoint Sophie. Yet at times, it occurs to me— what if I had stayed at Champs Blancs, relied on the discretion and generous spirit of the Merseys perhaps, and had the child myself? Sometimes my loneliness is unendurable when I think of myself alone in the world, having lost all who meant something to me. Would a child ease that suffering? But I have made a pact with Sophie, and as much as I fantasize about a little boy with eyes like his father, or a precious girl with dark curls like mine, I know it will not be. Not for me. Never for me.

Thursday, October 15th

The elixir that Sophie's doctor provided has done wonders. I barely know myself now, and live in a state of bliss. The nightmares have ceased and I find I am able to write in small snippets during the day, when I am not besieged by the attentions of Sophie and Sebastien. I feel as though I inhabit a dream, and time seems to pass by both quickly and slowly. I long for the freedom to wander the fields and hills of Champs Blancs, but for now, I bide my time and wait for the inevitable. I had a dream last night, more of a remembrance, of Lucius and I as children, lying on one of the hills that surround Champs Blancs. Nestled in the soft grass under a midsummer sun, we watch the clouds drift by lazily. He takes my hand and says to me, "I wish it could always be so—you and I, together in this place.

I reply, "I wish it too." His hand is like my own and our flesh becomes one.

He smiles and points. "That cloud looks like the castle we will build one day. We will live there together and have many horses, and ride every day. Would that not be lovely, Louisa?"

"Yes, so lovely." Then I feel the sun's warmth fading. I awake, tears in my eyes, weeping for what might have been, for all that I have lost.

Monday, November 2

I have no knowledge of the process of giving birth, and I admit to some trepidation. But Sophie has assured me that it is a most natural process and that she will be by my side the entire time, with Sebastien waiting in the wings. She has requested that I remain for a few weeks after the child is born to nurse it, and I have reluctantly agreed. After everything they have done for me, how could I say no? Champs Blancs will stay silent without me, although I cannot wait for the day I return and throw open the doors and windows, ready to cleanse both the house and myself of all the ghosts who haunt it—that is, if I can.

Chapter 15: Greta

In the silence that followed Michael's question, Greta heard a clock ticking from somewhere in the house. She was suddenly, inexplicably nervous. He was staring at her, waiting for a response, with such intensity that it was off-putting. Finally, she centred herself and smiled.

"Actually, I was hoping to see the letters first, if that's all right. I've been dying to read them, get a glimpse into the head of someone who may have been obsessed with Louisa Duberger, maybe find out more about her." Michael's smile dropped, and she quickly added, "It doesn't have to take long. I know you're anxious to keep exploring the house, but I really feel that I'd be in a better frame of mind if I knew what kind of things you'd already found." She paused, uneasy. Michael seemed almost angry and for a second, she thought he was going to refuse. But why? Why would he not want her to see the letters? As she was about to tell him not to worry about it, that she could see them later, he sighed.

"Of course, you're right. I can imagine how much you've been anticipating reading them. I forget that to me, they're old news. We don't have time for you to read through all of them, but yes, certainly, you can see them. They're just in my study." With that, he walked past her out of the kitchen. Greta assumed she was supposed to follow him, so she did, as he led her back through the hallway, out into the foyer, and through the door on the other side of the stairs. It opened into a large living room which was sparsely furnished, with old couches, a formica coffee table, and threadbare rugs.

"This is where the previous occupants spent most of their time," he said with distaste. "I haven't had a chance to tackle it yet, but you'll find my study quite cozy." He pointed at another door almost hidden in the wall. Greta went through and found herself in a small but well-decorated room. Michael was right; it *was* very cozy; there was a fireplace flanked by wingback chairs, a leather couch, and a large oak Mission-style desk in front of a large window.

"This is lovely," Greta said, walking to the window. It looked out onto a small courtyard surrounded by the house's walls on three sides. "What's that?" She pointed to a hatch that appeared to lead into the ground against the side of one wall.

"That? Just an access to the basement."

"A basement? I'd love to see that too," she commented, but Michael immediately shut the idea down, a little too aggressively, she thought.

"No, you absolutely can't go down there. It's...very damp and moldy. You might end up sick. Lots of spiders, which I'm sure you'd rather avoid."

Greta wasn't really bothered by spiders, or any insects really, but obviously Michael had been in the basement, and if it was as damp and moldy as he said, there wouldn't be anything worth salvaging, so she didn't pursue the idea.

"Here," he said, opening one of the desk drawers and producing a file folder. "Here are the letters. You can get a taste of them now and spend more time with them later, after we've done some work." He pulled a single sheet of paper out of the folder and passed it to her.

Greta was a little annoyed by his attitude—he was acting as if he was in charge of her time. But then again, she thought, he was giving her the kind of access to research that students only dreamed about, even if it was in dribs and drabs. She took the piece of paper Michael had given her over to the leather couch. The cushions were thick and soft, and she sank into its embrace, focused on the words on the page in front of her. She frowned. "This letter is typed. Did you transcribe the original?"

"The handwriting was hard to decipher. I have all the originals somewhere safe, don't worry. Read it out loud," Michael said. It sounded more like a command than a request and Greta stiffened, but he added, "I think it would be more impactful that way—you have a lovely voice."

She laughed self-consciously but cleared her throat and began. "'To the one who chains my soul.' There's no date—were you able to put these in some kind of chronological order?"

"Yes, yes, as best I could," Michael said impatiently. "Continue."

"'Upon this page, I declare my love for you, a deep, passionate adoration for you. Yet you give me no reply, save to shun my presence. Oh L. you know that living without you would destroy me. Do you not remember your vow? I know that we were children but I am as sincere now as if I possessed the wisdom of the ages. How can you think to leave me for—what? The promise of an empty life away from the joy we have known together here? Shall I rend my garments? Tear out my hair? Scream my love for you to all the devils in hell? Let me know that I may do it and be satisfied.' Wow," Greta breathed out. "Talk about obsessive. It's signed, 'The One Who Lives In Torment.' Are they all like this?"

Michael nodded. "Pretty much, from what I initially saw." He reached out his hand. Greta reluctantly gave him the letter, which he placed back in the file folder. He put the folder in his desk drawer. Then, "I don't know about 'obsessive,'" he said, almost gruffly, as he slid the drawer shut and locked it. "Some people might call it romantic. But you can look at them all more closely later at your leisure." He brightened. "Now that you've had your craving filled, are you ready to begin the quest?"

Greta sank back into the cushions and inwardly sighed, thinking it would be nice to just stay where she was and keep reading, but she responded, "Of course. Where should we start?"

"The attic. I hope you brought some old clothes—there are layers of dirt up there from the Iron Age, I'm sure," he quipped.

"Oh, damn, I didn't even think of that. It's not a problem—this outfit is pretty much wash and wear. No worries."

"Well, I *am* worried. I have a coverall around here somewhere you can put on. No, I insist!" he said, cutting off her protest. He hurried away, leaving Greta alone in the study shaking her head.

Julian was right—Michael really was old-fashioned, and more than a little eccentric, even controlling, as she'd initially thought. It grated on her nerves—she was no damsel in distress, needing a man to keep her safe—and clean too, apparently. She was anxious to get going, and here he was delaying on account of...what? A little dust?

But he was back a few minutes later, carrying a canvas onesie covered in paint splotches. "Here," he thrust it at her. "This'll do the trick."

Greta took the coverall, murmuring her thanks and stepped into it, pulling it up and then over her shoulders. It was large on her and she felt like a child playing dress-up as she waved the sleeves back and forth then rolled them up. Michael looked at her appraisingly. "That's better. Now you don't have to worry about ruining your lovely clothes. Right—come this way."

He took her on a meandering path through the vast house, out of the kitchen, up the main stairs, and then into his wing where, right at the end of the hallway, he stopped in front of a thick wooden door. "This leads up to the third floor—at one time it was the servants' quarters. Now it's mostly empty rooms used for storage, but from there, you'll see another door that accesses the attic proper. The stairs are steep so be careful," he cautioned.

They made their way through a dimly lit hallway. On either side, there were connected, derelict rooms with stark white walls and torn carpeting. A stack of old paintings leaned in the corner of one of the rooms, and Michael gestured to them. "Some of these are quite valuable. I'll be hanging them in the guest quarters once the renovations are complete. Imagine the quality of guests I'll have, all deserving of this type of luxury, once your research is complete and you've published your thesis about Louisa, her life and poetry, the letters, the romance. People will be fascinated."

Greta said nothing; it was clear that she and Michael had very different ideas about what was romantic and what wasn't, although he was correct in one regard—people would definitely be fascinated.

In another of the rooms, there were suitcases stacked on top of each other. "Haven't finished unpacking yet?" Greta paused and pointed at them.

"No, they're not mine. A few things the previous owners left behind, nothing important. Come on."

"So what are your plans for this part of the house?" she asked. "More guest rooms?"

Michael shook his head. "Just storage most likely. It's very hard to heat up here in the winter. And the lack of windows makes things a bit depressing, don't you think?" Without waiting for her to answer, he quickly changed the subject. "So, how long have you and...what was his name... Julian been engaged?"

Greta hesitated, mentally calculating. "Almost two years."

Michael made a scoffing sound. "Doesn't sound very serious. If it was me, I'd be rushing you to the altar!"

Greta laughed uncomfortably; Michael seemed to be honing into her own past misgivings about her fiancé, but still, she felt the need to defend Julian. "We're just waiting until we're financially more stable, that's all. Neither of us is in a 'rush.'"

Michael shrugged dismissively but said nothing else on the

subject. At last, they came to another, smaller door with an old-fashioned lock. He produced a skeleton key from his pocket and twisted it in the lock until they both heard an audible click.

"See this key?" he asked, taking it out of the lock and waving it in the air. "This key can lock or unlock any room in the house. Very handy." He pulled the door open. "I'd say 'after you,' but these stairs can be treacherous. Stay behind me...and catch me if I fall!" he laughed. He picked up an LED lantern that was sitting on the bottom step and turned it on. The beam wasn't very strong and Greta looked dubious.

"Don't worry," he said, swinging the lantern. "I've rigged utility lighting in the attic—this is just to get us up the stairs." They climbed the steps, Greta clutching the thin handrail, and when they got to the top, he instructed, "Stay here for a minute." He disappeared into the blackness. Greta followed the weak beam of light as it danced around the dark attic, then suddenly, the entire place was flooded with brightness and she squinted against it for a moment until her eyes adjusted. When they did, she gasped. The attic was as massive as the house itself, stretching far off into the distance. Heavy roof joists and support beams cast long shadows onto the half-walls and wooden floor, which was dotted with small puddles where the roof tiles were missing.

"Another thing to fix," Michael sighed, staring at the water pooling on the floor. "Over here—this is where I found the letters." He pointed to a cavity behind a section of wall that he had already demolished. "Amazing. I was looking for dead rats and found a treasure trove."

"How many letters were there altogether?"

"The handful you saw, maybe eight. But I'm sure there must be more."

Greta stared around the attic at all the other places where secrets could be hidden. It seemed almost daunting, but she was willing to give it a try. "Hopefully we can make some progress over the next day or two."

"Oh, I think it will take more than just a couple of days to search this space. You might end up being here for a while longer," Michael said matter-of-factly, bending down to open a toolbox.

Greta was taken aback. "But...I can't stay that long."

"Why not?" He took a crowbar out of the toolbox and came towards her. Greta instinctively stepped back, and he stopped. "I'm sure Julian can do without you for a little while. And this is really important."

"I know," Greta said, trying to sound reassuring. "It's just that my younger sister is staying with me, and I don't want her to worry. Our mother just passed away. Remember? The funeral was the other day." It was a bold lie—Helen surely wouldn't have cared if Greta dropped off the face of the earth, but it gave Michael pause.

"Let's see how far we get," he suggested, turning his back on her and heading towards a section of half-wall. He started using his crowbar to pry at the top of the wall boards, so Greta wandered around, making her way to the far corner, away from him.

She stared at the walls, overwhelmed. She'd been given no real direction—where should she even begin? Michael noticed that she hadn't moved. He stopped working and called out, "What's the matter?"

"I'm not actually sure what to do. Do you want me to look for loose boards or...do you have another crowbar?"

He laughed. "Sorry. I've been alone here for so long that sometimes I forget the social niceties. Yes, use the LED lantern to get up close and check for boards that seem a little loose or have a gap between them. If you find any, use...uh, use this prybar to pop the top trim off and then look down inside." He gestured at his toolbox. Greta gave him a thumbs up, made her way over to the toolbox and grabbed the prybar. There was a lot of debris on the floor of the attic, splintered wood and what looked like pieces of broken roof slates, she thought, from the way they crunched under her feet. She was wearing running shoes—she hoped there were no roofing nails lurking under the rubble.

Carefully, she began to scan the walls, holding the lantern up in front of her. The walls were built from pine, attached vertically to create a board and batten-style wainscotting, topped with pieces of wide flat trim, creating a hollow space between the inner and outer walls deep enough to hide all kinds of things. The boards seemed very sturdy and she tapped a few with the prybar—they were firmly in place. But then, as she moved along towards the corner, the light from the LED glinted against a finishing nail and she realized that there was a slight gap between two of the boards and the trim. She didn't want to get Michael's hopes up, so she didn't say anything. She shoved the prybar under the section of the top board and levered it until it inched up slightly, the nails squealing. She moved further along and continued to pry until the top board was loose enough that she could use her hands to pull it off. Breathlessly, she picked up the lantern and peered into the depths of the dead space.

"Ew!" she exclaimed. Michael looked in her direction and dropped his crowbar, about to rush over, but she waved him off. "I think I found your dead rat," she said, shuddering at the sight of the small skeleton. "I wonder how it managed to get in here." She shone the beam on an angle, trying to see the bottom of the cavity. "Looks like he chewed through one of the joists that divide the sections of wall. There's a hole at the bottom—," she started, then stopped as something else caught her eye. Peeking out from the hole that led into the next section of wall was the corner of a piece of paper.

Chapter 16: Louisa
1891

Thursday, December 24th

I find myself overcome with sadness today. Christmas Eve is upon us and I miss the celebrations that we used to have at Champs Blancs when Mother was alive. On Christmas Eve, we would feast on roast goose, and then we would go to church and listen to Pastor Campbell relate the Christmas story, spellbound and overcome with the joy of the season as we sang carols until midnight. Then home in the horse-drawn sleigh, huddled together for warmth, Lucius and I arm-in-arm under our cloaks on one side, and Mother and Father, merry and rosy-cheeked, on the other side, whispering to each other and laughing as we sped through the drifts. Then to bed, but scarcely able to sleep. I would creep out of my chambers and sneak into Lucius's room; there we would snuggle together under that warmth of the covers, whispering excitedly, anticipating the morning and what presents we may receive from Father Christmas, until our eyes became heavy and we drifted off. Lucius longed for a new hunting rifle, while I had my heart set on books. I could almost weep, envisioning the two of us, innocents still, full of hope and good cheer.

Now of course, I am alone, sequestered in the silence of my room. Earlier, Sophie presented me with a volume of Miss Emily Dickinson's poetry, as well as a tray of oranges and other treats— fudge, marzipan, and toffees, which I received with as much jubilation as I could muster. There is a party downstairs but I may not be seen, and spend this holiest of holy nights in solitude, praying that the child within me will know such joy as I had once known on the eve of our Saviour's birth. For me, there will be only hellfire and scorn. Yet what if I should appear? I am sorely tempted to chance the scandal and reveal myself for the sinful creature I am, but I must not. Sebastien and Sophie have been my loving jailors for these many months, caring for me when no one else would. I must refrain from these urges, stay focused on the child and its well-being, until it is time to deliver it unto the world as Mary did her own beloved son.

1892

Monday, February 16th

It is done. I have delivered the child and am now recovering from the ordeal. My labour was long and hard, made even more so by Sebastien's insistence that I refrain from crying out as best I could, as the servants could distinguish my voice from Sophie's. The midwife was a decrepit woman, chosen for her ability to maintain discretion if paid handsomely, and she provided neither the expertise nor care that a woman in my position would require. Sophie stood by, anxious and pacing the length of the room, while Sebastien waited in the corridor as was proper. The pain was great—at one point, I fear I fainted, but the midwife gave my face such a slap that my head rang. At least it was a distraction from the agony of labour. Finally, the child emerged and the relief was palpable. A brief cry and then the midwife: "A boy". He was cleaned and swaddled and whisked away by Sophie without my ever seeing him. I could hear Sebastien and Sophie outside my room—their elation was a comfort. If nothing else, I have at least guaranteed a good life for this child.

Later, after the midwife had completed her ministrations and departed, Sophie brought the child to me to nurse. I could not bear to look at him, and closed my eyes while she unbuttoned my gown and nestled him in my bosom. The sensation was indescribable, and I began to weep.

"Sister, do not despair," she said. "You have given us the greatest gift, yet you will not be unknown to this child. You will be Aunt Louisa, and you will always have a place at Maison de Lierre."

"What shall you name him?" I asked.

"We have decided on 'Louis.'"

Louis? It is a good name, and fitting. He will know me only as Aunt Louisa, and I shall love him as best I can.

"And Louisa," Sophie continued to console me. "Do not fret. Sebastien has found a wet nurse. You may only be required to feed the child for two more weeks, and then she will take on the task. It seemed the best course—I must be in society and cannot be confined for any longer. I'm sure you understand. And once she has arrived, you may choose to stay on for a while—or return to Champs Blancs ...if you so desire."

The unspoken caution hung in the air. They would prefer me to go, and leave them to take on their parental roles without interference. "A sound plan," I concurred. "Although I would like to return on occasion to see the child. I would not—I would never—reveal myself to him. But, an aunt, as you say—surely he could benefit from an additional loving family connection."

Sophie hesitated then spoke. "I trust in you, Louisa, and know you would never breach the oath that you swore. Yes, you may indeed visit. It would do little Louis good to have a kind aunt such as yourself to look forward to seeing. I myself had a dowager aunt who came to stay every summer who brought me gifts and made herself my favourite...after my own mother of course. You shall be welcome in the same vein."

"I thank you," I said, and I was not dissembling. I am truly grateful to my cousins for their generosity of spirit and I will be glad to return to Champs Blancs. Perhaps now that this sordid episode is almost over, I can attempt to live a life of quiet solitude back at my home. For the present, I will endeavour to refrain from looking at little Louis or touching him, so that I may never feel the bond that a mother and child share. That bond is for Sophie. Not for me. Never for me.

Tuesday, March 1ˢᵗ

The wet nurse has arrived, a woman close in age to Sophie but whose husband is employed at Sebastien's factory and welcomes the income from his wife's profession. They have several children of their own, the oldest of whom will care for the youngest, who has just now been weaned, while their mother resides at Maison de Lierre. It seems a complicated affair when I could continue the task myself, but Sophie made it very clear, albeit with a gentleness and compassion for my situation, that she and Sebastien would prefer that I return to Champs Blancs and leave them to bond with the child. Louis is a lovely infant, with a cap of dark hair and dark eyes—Sophie says he must take after me, he resembles me so closely. But Sebastien also possesses the same Duberger dark looks, and there shall certainly be no speculation as to the child's parentage.

The train tickets have been purchased and I depart on the morrow. What little effects I own, I have packed in my small valise—I leave with hardly more than I came with, save for the volume of Miss Dickinson's poetry which has been some comfort to me these last few months. I have messaged ahead to Pastor Campbell, and he has kindly agreed to send a carriage to take me home when I arrive at the station. As much as I've longed for Champs Blancs, I also dread returning to the house, to the scene of such calamity. I have no real income, aside from the monthly allowance that Sebastien has graciously offered, and hope that I can exist on that. If all else fails, I can perhaps sell off some of the land—there is acreage beyond the hills that is workable and suited for farming. These decisions I shall make upon my return.

Now that I am no longer with child and can wear my corsets, I am allowed to appear in company. Tonight, there will be a celebration—Louis is to be presented to a small gathering of friends and neighbours of my hosts, who have been most excited to see the babe. It will be a brief appearance, however; the delivery took its toll on my body and I am only able to sit in a chair for short periods of time. Lying down eases the discomfort, and, if I am being completely honest, it will also be difficult to witness the small audience shower Sophie with the attention I might have had under different circumstances. I know both my cousins are relieved that I will dutifully be playing the role of the doting aunt, soon to be on my way and out of their lives for the time being. I feel their eyes on me sometimes, as if they are worried that I will break my promise and make a declaration that might ruin everything. Little do they know, I have no intentions of any kind. I would be the more ruined if the truth ever came to light.

Wednesday, March 2nd

I write this on the train, speeding away from Montreal and heading towards...what? I already feel a sense of isolation, a creeping loneliness, the further I move away from Maison de Lierre. Sebastien has paid for a Pullman car, which allows me to recline whenever needed, and I have no seatmate so that I might make full use of the space. The porter, thanks to a very large gratuity paid in advance by my cousin, has made up the bed and provided me with food and tea. I must seem a sight to those who pass by— lying in bed in the middle of the afternoon—but they assume I am ill and must rest. I *look* ill—I have lost considerable weight and the shadows under my eyes are dark against my pale skin.

Saying goodbye to Louis was difficult. I have endeavoured not to become attached to him, yet still I felt a tugging at my heart when I left him behind in the arms of his 'mother.' She will be good to him, I have no doubt, and will love him as her own— indeed, she demonstrated her commitment to him last evening. I have never seen a more proud mama, as she carried him close to her, showing him off to the guests, while I sat in the corner observing. I was introduced to the gathering as Cousin Louisa, but who would always be known as 'Aunt,' so fond was Sophie of me. "What a lucky auntie you are," one matron observed, "having this little darling to dote over!" and I replied in the affirmative as enthusiastically as I could.

But it is finished now, the whole ordeal behind me. My only desire is to forget all that has happened, to begin again with a clean slate, so that the next time I see Louis, I *will* be the doting aunt, and he and I will have an affectionate relationship that does not detract from the bond Sophie will develop with him.

Thursday, March 3rd

The journey was over almost as soon as it had begun. The train was much more quiet on the trip back, and I confess I slept soundly, thanks to the elixir, several bottles of which Sophie gifted to me before I departed. Indeed, the porter had to rouse me for breakfast, a plate of sausage, eggs, and bread. I was not able to eat much; my appetite is small these days, regardless of how tempting the repast. When we arrived at the station, Pastor Campbell was there himself to meet me. When I descended the train, he rushed to greet me and exclaimed in shock, "My dear! Are you unwell? I prayed that such a long visit to your cousins would restore you, but—and pardon me for saying, you look rather worse for wear."

"Oh no, I am perfectly fine," I insisted. "I have been missing home dreadfully and am positive the fresh air of Champs Blancs will be the cure I need." This latter was a lie sprung from hope, but it seemed to satisfy the Pastor. We chatted about inconsequential things for a great portion of the journey but as we drew closer to home, I began to feel a sense of unease. Then, upon reaching the verge of the hill overlooking Champs Blancs, I saw the house again for the first time in nearly a year. A darkness came over me and I began to tremble. Pastor Campbell was most disturbed and insisted that I return with him to the manse, but I thanked him for his concern and stated that I was only tired from the journey. He accepted my excuse, advising me to get some rest once at home, and informed me that he had arranged for the local grocer to provide me with deliveries each week to save me from the long walk into town. If I needed anything else, he directed me, I need only send word. Would he be so kind if he knew the true reason for my discomfiture?

As our carriage approached the house, we went by the ruined stable, its stone foundation intact despite the fire that had consumed the rest of the structure. I held my breath, trying to control the images that were threatening to invade my mind, and was almost successful...until we passed the well. As I stared, Lucius appeared, standing next to it, glaring back at me, blood dripping down his forehead, and I squeezed my eyes tight against the horrible sight. When I reopened them, he was gone.

Chapter 17: Greta

She shoved the prybar under the next piece of top trim and started heaving. Michael strode over and added his strength to the effort. The board flew up and then clattered to the ground. Michael grabbed the lantern and pointed the beam down into the hollow.

"Can you reach it?" he asked, excitedly. "Your arms are thinner than mine. If not, I can pull the whole wall apart."

"I think I can!" Greta plunged her arm into the gap, praying there were no more decomposing rats at the bottom. She felt around and her fingers rippled against several sheets of paper. She stood on her tiptoes, leaned over further, and was able to grab the sheaf, extracting it carefully so as not to drop it. Finally, her arm was free and she held the papers up to the light.

"Bring them here," he beckoned, already on his way over to a table in the middle of the attic directly underneath one of the bright utility lights. He pushed aside some tools and gestured for her impatiently to place the papers on the table. Greta put them down and spread them out carefully.

"The ink is faded, but there's definitely handwriting on these," she said. Michael picked up one of the pieces of paper and held it up to better catch the light. "What does it say?"

Michael breathed in deeply, exhilarated. "'A hundred days are one dark night/And all is black that once was white/For those of us without an aim/Where life and death seem all the same.' Can you believe it?"

"That's one of the pieces from *Peruse No Epitaph Upon My Grave*—I'm sure of it!" Greta exclaimed.

"There's no question. I know that volume like the back of my hand. This is the original—written by Louisa Duberger herself. It must be!"

Greta flipped through the rest of the papers gently, recognizing other lines from Louisa Duberger's poetry. "But why do you think she hid these in the walls? They were all published before she died. What was she trying to keep secret?" She pulled another piece of paper out of the stack and quickly scanned it while Michael was holding one of the poems up to the light. Her eyes opened wide in astonishment. "Michael, it's another letter to The One Who Chains My Soul"—she continued scanning, then gasped—"and it proves that Louisa *was* related to the person who was obsessed with her! Listen." She began to read out loud. "'Shared blood and bone'...'More than sibling love'? Not only were they related, it sounds like they were brother and sister. Did Louisa have a brother?" Greta looked at Michael, expectantly. He stared back at her, the look on his face inscrutable. She started flipping rapidly through the poetry, examining the pages. "I don't understand—this is the same handwriting. Could this letter and these poems all have been written by Louisa Duberger? Could she have been—"

As she said it, Michael reached over and roughly snatched the letter out of her hand. "Give that to me! I haven't had a chance to—"

"To what? What's wrong?" she asked, surprised.

He smiled tightly and gathered up the rest of the papers. "Nothing." With that, he turned and went towards the attic door, disappearing down the stairs, leaving her alone.

Greta was dumbfounded. She waited a few minutes, but there was no indication that Michael was planning to return, so she left the attic. She wandered through the third floor quietly, listening for any sounds of movement, but there were none. She shrugged to herself and continued down to Michael's wing. Still no sign of her host. She finally found him back in his study, sitting at his desk, lost in thought.

"Are you sure everything's all right?" she asked. He looked up as if seeing her for the first time. "Michael?"

He snapped out of his reverie and smiled, this time looking more relaxed. "It's nothing, really. I'm just a little overwhelmed, that's all. Like I said, I'm not used to having other people around. And I wanted to look at everything myself first. I've... never been very good at sharing." He gave a small laugh, and stood up. "I can't believe I found these with your help. We make a good team, don't we?" He sounded almost plaintive, as if he expected her to disagree.

"Uh, yeah, sure we do. So did you want to read them all through while I keep searching the attic? Then we can take a closer look at the poems and letters side by side, see if the handwriting really is the same?" Greta fully expected him to say no, or delay her from examining them more carefully, and he didn't disappoint.

"Actually, it's getting late. Why don't we go into town, have a little dinner at that café I told you about. They're open until 9, and they make the best risotto—really, you won't believe it."

He continued rambling on about the menu at the café until finally Greta said, "Okay, it sounds like a great place to eat. Just let me change out of these coveralls first."

"Sure. I'll pull the car 'round front and we can leave as soon as you're ready."

Greta went upstairs to her 'chambers' as Michael liked to call them, frustrated with his bizarre attitude and his fixation on getting dinner. At least she could call Julian once they got to the restaurant, she thought. She shut the door to her room and stripped off the coverall. She was actually glad Michael had insisted she wear it; it was covered in dust, but her clothes underneath had withstood the attic adventure without incident. She bundled the coverall up, intending to take it down with her to shake it off outside, then sat on the edge of the bed. The strange stain on the floor fascinated her. What could have caused it? It couldn't have been water damage—there were two more storeys above her, and if everything was leaking so badly, the attic and the third floor would have shown signs of water stains too. It was obviously embedded right into the oak grain, deep enough that even a powerful sanding couldn't completely remove it. If she squinted and turned down the lights, it would almost look like a pool of...blood. She shuddered and stood up. Suddenly, the room began to spin, disorienting her, and she sat back down hard on the bed. From somewhere, she could hear the rushing of water, overwhelming her; her vision began to dim and for a moment, she thought she smelled something putrid. She took a deep breath and shook her head until it cleared. *Too much excitement*, she thought, waiting until she regained her equilibrium. Once she was feeling more herself, she left the room, avoiding looking at the stain on the floor. Michael was right; it *was* disturbing.

When she got to the front door, Michael was waiting with the car running. It was an old Chrysler Neon, with rust on the side panels. Maybe he was one of those rich guys who didn't care about cars, she thought. Because the way he was talking to Julian, he should have been able to afford a Lamborghini. She opened the car door and caught a whiff of stale food, like take-out gone bad.

"Good to go?" he asked. She nodded. "You look lovely, by the way."

She slid into the passenger seat. "Thanks. Just the same thing I had on this morning. This isn't a fancy place, is it?"

"Oh no—very casual. You'll fit right in."

The ride into town was silent. Greta was unsure what topics of discussion might be off-limits based on Michael's behaviour earlier, and he didn't seem inclined to talk. She wanted to ask him more about Louisa, and the family, how he found the house, but she thought it would be better to wait until they were at the restaurant—maybe some risotto and wine would loosen him up a little, the way it had in Toronto.

The café was on the main street of town, tucked in between a bicycle repair shop and a convenience store. Inside, the décor was fairly standard, with small tables covered in red and white checkered tablecloths. It was bright, almost too bright, with banks of fluorescent bulbs giving everything a slightly green tinge.

They were greeted by a middle-aged woman wearing a uniform, who gave them a cheerful hello and said, "Feel free to sit anywhere." She was standing behind the counter next to a built-in showcase full of pie slices on plates—there was a large variety to choose from, just as Michael had said. They had their pick of tables—it was so late that there were no other patrons—and he led Greta to the corner by the window.

"You won't be too chilly here, will you?" he asked. "I like this table the best—great view of the street."

The waitress came over with a couple of menus, but Michael waved her off, and she tucked them under her arm, smiling. "Don't tell me—let me guess. The risotto, right?"

Michael nodded. "Make it two. And a bottle of the house red." Greta was annoyed again—she wasn't a huge fan of risotto and had wanted to see the menu for herself, but she shrugged inwardly. At least there was wine. The waitress quickly brought a bottle and opened it for them. Michael made a big show of swirling it around his glass, sniffing it, and then inhaling deeply before taking a sip and pronouncing it 'fine.' Greta tried not to laugh at his pretension—after all, it was a cheap brand not a Chateau Lafite—but she smiled graciously when he poured her a glass. "A toast," he said, holding his glass up. Greta did the same. "To the thrill of discovery." They clinked glasses and Greta took it as an opening.

"Speaking of discoveries, what do you think about those letters and the poetry? Could they actually be written by the same person? I mean, do you think Louisa wrote all of them? And if it *was* her, who was *she* obsessed with?"

Michael took a sip of wine. "It couldn't have been her. People back then were all taught the same style of cursive handwriting. It's just a coincidence. Or...someone else made copies of the poems, the same someone who wrote the letters. It could even have been a servant, writing about his unrequited love for someone he worked for."

"But you're discounting the 'sibling' angle. Did Louisa have a brother? What if she was obsessed with *him*? Ooh," she continued, getting excited, "what if—"

"Stop!" Michael hissed. "Enough." He sat back in his chair, obviously fuming. "Try to understand—this is my *family* you're talking about. Louisa was my great-great AUNT. I don't want to hear anymore about it. It's preposterous!" He tossed back the wine in his glass and hastily poured himself another. "You know, I really thought we were a team, that you were going to help me control the narrative." He gulped some more wine, then put down the glass and stared at her, his arms crossed over his chest.

"What do you mean, 'control the narrative'? What narrative?"

He leaned forward and spoke in a low, angry voice. "I'm trying to build something here, Greta, a legacy, a family history, something that I can use to create a successful business model. Imagine it—a beautiful inn, a destination centre, maybe even a writer's retreat for people who want to immerse themselves in the life of a 19th century poet. Your research, that PhD—when it's published—could help me make sure that the inn, and Louisa, become famous for the *right* reasons, and no one would question *any* of it! How many people do you think will come if that writer was raped by her brother—and the rest of the entire family line, including the owner of the inn, was the product of incest?!"

Greta was astounded by his outburst. "You *knew*," she said slowly and quietly. "All this time you knew and you lied to me? What else did you find?!"

"Dinner is here. Eat your risotto."

Greta didn't know what to say, so she said nothing. The waitress arrived with two steaming plates of risotto and a small wicker basket heaped with rolls. Greta ignored the food and pulled her phone out of her bag, remembering that the café had free wifi. There was a sign on the wall with the password, and she logged in.

"What are you doing?" Michael asked tersely.

"I'm calling my fiancé. Letting him know that I'm okay. And that he can come pick me up first thing in the morning." She disregarded the disdainful sneer on Michael's face and looked at her phone screen, which was suddenly flooded with text messages as the wifi kicked in. All from Julian. All "Call me as soon as you can". Her stomach did a flip—had something happened to him? She clicked on his name in her contacts, already imagining the worst—he'd been in an accident on the way home, the antique market had gotten robbed and he was hurt, stabbed, shot—when Julian answered right away, she was flooded with relief.

"Greta, I'm so happy to hear your voice. Is everything all right?"

"Well—" she pushed her chair out and was just about to move away somewhere more private when he interrupted.

"Is that guy with you right now? Just say yes or no."

Greta was confused, but did as Julian told her. "Yes."

"Can he hear you?"

"Not really. We're just sitting here at dinner."

"Okay. I have to tell you something and it's really important that you don't react. Just smile and say, I understand."

"I don't—"

"Greta, please!"

"I understand." She tried to smile convincingly.

"After the market closed, I had a little free time—I got to thinking about what he'd said about selling his company and being rich and all that. I was bored without you, so I tried to look him up. I couldn't find anything at first, at least nothing under the name Michael Shepherd. But then I went to Google images and saw a picture of a guy who kind of resembled him, taken a few years ago. There was an article—again, it's really important that you don't react to this—about him, but his name wasn't Michael Shepherd, it was Michel Duberger. I checked—'Duberger' is French and it translates into 'Shepherd.' And the article? It was all about how this tech guy had stalked his ex-wife until she got a restraining order. A month later she called 911, told them he was outside her house... then she disappeared. So did he. There's a warrant out for him in Quebec."

Greta's eyes opened wide and she looked at Michael. "What's

wrong?" he asked.

"Nothing—uh, Julian's store got broken into," she impro-
vised. "But no one was hurt." Michael grunted and turned away.
Greta said quietly into the phone, "Where are you? It sounds like
you're driving."

"I am. I'm coming to get you. Right now."

Chapter 18: Louisa
1892

Wednesday, March 16th

It has been almost two full weeks since I returned home to Champs Blancs. I find myself wandering the corridors aimlessly, at loose ends, and fearful of what I may find lurking around the corners. I had grown used to Sophie and Sebastien—even as I was confined to my chambers, they visited me regularly. Sophie often stayed during the afternoons, and we would read together or sew. Sebastien would bring me books, but once he discovered that I wrote poetry, he gifted me with a finely bound leather journal that I am using to create my newest collection. Perhaps one day, I will have them published for Louis to read when he is older and I am long gone—I hope he will not think ill of me, as these pieces represent my darkest of thoughts. Today, however, he is one month old and I find myself wondering about him. What can infants do at one month of age? Can he smile yet? Can he tell the difference between my bosom and the wet nurse's? Does he smile at *her*?

The vision I had of Lucius by the well continues to haunt me, and I have seen him again, out there and also in the house. He stalks the hallway between our chambers—I hear his steps echoing—and I catch glimpses of him in the parlour right before I go in, but when I arrive, he has vanished from sight. My mind is unstable, that is the rational explanation...or is he here to torment me, sent by the devil himself as retribution for what I have done? I have scrubbed the floor of my chamber over and over again, yet the stain will not be removed. It is a constant reminder of my guilt and shame, and I have taken to sleeping in Father's room. I know that Father's soul is not trapped on this plane—I have called out to him, begged for a sign, yet he speaks not. Regardless, I know that he would forgive me if he knew of my sins, even if I can never forgive myself.

Sunday, March 20th

In the time before everything fell into calamity, I would have just arrived home from church instead of remaining in my night-clothes all morning. I have not the strength to dress, so imagine my horror when the bell rang. I had just taken a delivery from the grocer on Friday; he was the only one who regularly came to the house, but he did not expect me to receive him. I declined to answer, but then the most terrible knocking began. I peered from an upstairs window, hidden behind the curtain, and saw the landau belonging to the Merseys parked in the drive. Mrs. Mersey herself was calling upon me! I scarcely knew what to do—I ran to my closet and threw on a duster to give the pretence that I had been occupied with cleaning, then hastened down the stairs and opened the door, just as she was about to leave. She turned, surprised, then her surprise turned to shock.

"Louisa?" she asked. "I scarcely recognize you!" She approached and touched my cheek. "Are you ill? My dear girl, what has happened to you?"

I fought futilely to find the words to answer her, then finally burst into tears. She took my arm and led me back into the house, instructing her driver to wait for her. We sat down together in the parlour, and we remained in silence until I had regained my composure.

"It is most kind of you to visit, I am sure," I said. "I have not seen many people since I returned home from my cousins." I gestured at my costume. "I have been attempting to clean Father's room. It is a consuming task with no servants to assist, and I have not yet had the time to hire any."

If she doubted my explanation, she was too much a gentlewoman to say so. Instead, she let me retain what little dignity I had left, and simply replied, "Of course. What an awful thing to have to do. You must be exhausted. Indeed, you look it. Let me send for the doctor, I insist."

"No, please!" I exclaimed. "I have no need. I have an elixir that helps with my nerves, although I have precious few drops left...." It was true. The last bottle of the several I brought with me from Maison de Lierre was almost empty, forcing me to ration the remainder.

"What elixir?" she demanded. "Bring it to me that I may see what you have been prescribed."

I hurried to my room and retrieved the bottle from the bedside table. When she looked at the label, she gasped. "Louisa! How long have you been taking this? It is a most powerful medicine, containing opium. Who ordered it for you?"

"My cousin gave it to me. To help me sleep. After all that had occurred before my visit, he and his wife simply wanted to ease my sorrow."

"Well, this is a most unhealthy way to grieve. How irresponsible of your cousins to provide you with something so dangerous. But I fear if you stop taking it now, you will suffer more greatly. I will return on the morrow with another bottle, and instructions from the doctor regarding the cessation of such a treatment. I only wish I had thought to visit you sooner."

She put on her gloves and prepared to leave but I leapt up. "How—how is Tomas? Has he been well during my absence?"

She paused and her face flushed slightly. "Tomas? Did Pastor Campbell not tell you?" I shook my head no. "Tomas has married, my dear," she said softly. "To Sylvia Montgomery. I am sorry for it. I had had such hopes for a match between the two of you—" She stopped speaking, the unspoken "but" hanging in the air between us. I turned away, stifling the tears that threatened to fall anew.

"Of course he has wed," I said with my back to her. "He is a most courteous gentleman and deserves every happiness."

"He walked down the aisle with a red ribbon hidden in his waistcoat pocket," she whispered, her voice catching. "I will be back tomorrow. I promise." And then she was gone.

Tomas Mersey, married. Once again, my heart breaks for those things that, because of Lucius, were not meant for me. Never for me. I see Lucius standing there, in the parlour, his arms out to me, beseeching, and I throw a vase from the hall table at him. It smashes into a million pieces, each of which transform into droplets of water that begin to swirl and boil, and then he disappears into the whirlpool. But I will see him again. I have no doubt of that.

*Monday, March 21*st

As promised, Mrs. Mersey returned this morning. I had washed and dressed, and pinned up my hair for the occasion, but when she rang the bell, I hid once again behind the upstairs curtains, waiting for her to leave. I could not face her, could not bear to see the kindness in her eyes, and the pity there as well. She commenced knocking, but after several minutes, she gave up. She was holding a bottle and an envelope. She put the bottle down on the stoop, and took a pencil from her bag, spending several moments writing something on the back of the envelope, which she placed next to the bottle. She drove away, but I waited until the landau had disappeared over the crest of the hill before I went downstairs and opened the door.

I picked up the large medicine bottle and tucked it into my dress pocket. Next to the bottle was an envelope embossed with the name of the local doctor, Dr. Fowler. On the back, Mrs. Mersey had written the following: "Dearest Louisa, I am most sorry that you are not entertaining visitors today. Please accept this prescription of Montague's Soothing Syrup, as well as instructions from Dr. Fowler as to dosage and usage. When you are feeling less indisposed, send word and I will gladly come again. Yours, Eliza Mersey."

I threw the envelope onto the table without reading the contents, opened the bottle and drank until I was numb. It is now evening and my senses have started to revive. I cannot say which is better: to live somnolent with my senses dulled, or to be tormented by the ghosts who haunt me.

Tuesday, March 22nd

A letter came today from Maison de Lierre. It was an invitation from Sophie and Sebastien to attend the christening of Louis on Sunday next. The invitation was couched in cautions; I had only just returned home, the trip was long and arduous, and so on. But the invitation was extended to visit during the summer, when the weather was more conducive to travel. I have spent the last two days in a stupor and am in no fit condition to make the journey regardless, and although I feel almost desperate to see Louis once more, I think it best to wait, as my cousins have suggested, until the summer time. Then perhaps, if all is well, I may visit over Christmas and then again for his first birthday. I invited the young man who delivered the letter into the hall to await a reply, which I wrote hastily. I declined to attend the christening with regret—I was overwhelmed with finalizing Father's affairs, attending to the property and chattels, and making plans to hire staff. My cousins need not know that there were no affairs to settle, that the property goes on with or without my interference and as for chattels, there are also none. Regarding the hiring of staff, I have no such plans, lacking the income to do so. Since I cannot jeopardize the allowance that Sebastien, without knowing it, holds over my head, if they would prefer me to wait before returning, then wait I shall. Perhaps if I abide by their timelines, they will see that I am no trouble and that I will not interfere.

And I have made a firm decision. In order to present myself

in the best possible way to Louis, and ensure an ongoing schedule of visits, I have locked the bottle of laudanum syrup in the drawer of Father's desk, and will abstain from taking it. My recovery will be painful, but no more painful than the thought of never seeing Louis again.

Thursday, June 30th

Pastor Campbell will be arriving soon, to take me by carriage to the train station. I am to stay with my cousins for two weeks—a trial visit to ensure that they remain secure in my discretion. I am in the correct frame of mind now for such a journey, having recovered completely from my need for Montague's Soothing Syrup. It was an agonizing trial: my body ached and my mind was in disarray for many days. I'm still not certain what was worse—the physical pain or the mental torment of seeing Lucius at every turn, his face bloody and his arms reaching out to me—but the symptoms of the withdrawal gradually subsided and my glimpses of my brother are only fleeting, as if he were just on the edge of my vision. I put this diary in its safe haven, well-hidden under the floorboards of my bedchamber until you, the reader of the future, may find it and know the truth, or until I have need to write to you once more. For now, all I will do is to pray to become the cherished aunt to a child who knows me only thus. It is not the role I choose, but I shall play the part, as I have played many others over the years. And one day, Louis may come to Champs Blancs and I will see it anew, through his innocent eyes.

I have closed up the house until I return, and have said my goodbyes to Mrs. Mersey, who has become a true friend to me, despite the troubled beginnings of our relationship. She visits regularly and has proven to be most helpful regarding the sale of a few acres of land, which will allow me to maintain Champs Blancs and live there in some comfort. Lucius will, of course, come with me—no matter where I flee, he follows. I do believe he will be with me for the rest of this life and into the next. As for you, dear reader, I bid you adieu—at least

Chapter 19: Greta

The drive home was tense. Michael had refused to elaborate further at dinner about his shocking revelation concerning Louisa, and asked for the bill the second he had put the last forkful of risotto in his mouth. He'd consumed most of the bottle of wine, and although he seemed steady on his feet, Greta was still nervous. She'd offered to drive, but he turned her down brusquely.

It was dark when they arrived at Champs Blancs. The car stopped abruptly in front of the stone steps with a squeal of the brakes. In the time between leaving the café and coming back to the house, Michael had gotten progressively more unsteady, or at least it seemed that way to Greta, who saw him stagger when he got out of the car. She went on ahead, but then had to wait awkwardly for him to unlock the door. Once he did, she stormed past him.

"Where are you going?" he demanded, his voice slurring slightly.

"Up to my room, that's all. I'm tired." She reached the bottom of the stairs and heard his footsteps behind her. She panicked for a moment, but then he turned off and headed towards his study. She breathed a sigh of relief—*Julian, where are you?* she thought, then began immediately to worry. How would Michael react when Julian arrived on his doorstep and rang the bell? She went into her room and locked the door behind her just in case.

She spent some time packing her things into her overnight bag, but there was still no sign of Julian. Why wasn't he here yet? She was feeling decidedly panicky, and sat on the bed, trying to calm her breathing. What if he couldn't find the turn in the dark? She checked her phone, wishing she could call him, that some miracle would happen and she would see full bars, but there was nothing, no way to communicate with him. She walked to the window and peered out, searching for headlights breaking through the black night when, without warning, her bedroom door flew open. She turned, startled, and Michael was standing there, grinning and waggling his skeleton key at her. He was swaying slightly. He pocketed the key and then picked up a scotch glass full of liquor from the hallway floor. He looked over at the bed where her overnight bag sat, packed.

"What do you think you're doing?" He drained the glass of scotch, took a wobbling step into the room, and slammed the glass down hard on a side table. Greta moved from the window to the other side of the bed, keeping it in between them.

"I t-told you," she stammered. "Julian is coming to pick me up in the morning."

"No, he's not," Michael laughed. "I heard everything you said to him on the phone. I was sitting right there, remember? You never said anything to him about wanting to leave. Anyway, you're not going anywhere. It took a lot for me to get you here, and I'm not letting you go."

Greta's blood ran cold. "What are you talking about?"

"I knew it, from the minute I saw your name in the binder at the library that we shared a special connection. And when you agreed to come here, I knew you felt it too." He took another teetering step forward, grabbing at a chair with one hand. "But now—I can see that you're just like all the others. You don't care about me. All you care about is exposing the truth and ruining me. And you know the worst part? You were right. It's all true."

Greta realized that he was gripping a bound leather journal in his other hand, with papers tucked inside it, papers she assumed were the poetry and letters from the attic. "What's true?"

He groaned and waved the book at her. "See this? D'you know what this is?" Greta shook her head silently. "It's a diary. *Louisa's* diary. Can you believe it?"

Greta swallowed hard. *Keep him talking*, she thought. "Where did you find it? Was it in the attic too?"

"No! It was in here. Hidden under the floor, just like her poem said: 'My life is buried under oak.' She didn't say *in* oak, like a coffin—*under* it. I found it when I was trying to get that bloodstain out of the floor, trying to make the room nice for *you*! The sander got caught on a nail and when I realized one of the floorboards was loose, I lifted it up. This was hidden in there. Just. Like. The. Poem. Crazy, right?"

"And what does her diary say?" She tried to keep the quiver out of her voice.

"I told you. It's all true. Obsession, rape, murder—it's a family curse, that's for sure. But you—you can help me. It doesn't have to be like this. We don't have to say who the letters were from. We can say whatever we want! There was another man she talked about in the diary, Tomas Mersey—we can say it was him. We can turn it into a romance, like the Brownings, instead of some sordid scandal. Please!"

Greta shook her head slowly. "I'm sorry. There's such a thing as academic integrity. And I can't publish something I know is a lie."

"And I can't let you publish the truth. I really hoped that I could trust you, but I was wrong, so..." He giggled drunkenly and reached into his pocket. "Too bad no one will ever know about it." Greta thought he was going to take out the skeleton key, lock her in, but instead, he pulled out a lighter.

Greta's eyes widened in fear. "Michael, what are you doing?" She moved slightly closer to the nightstand next to the bed where a large bronze candlestick holder sat, its intricate base carved with cherubs. One more step sideways and it would be within reach.

"The same thing that Great-Great... Great? I always lose track of the greats... Grandmother did. Burn it all down. Starting with this." He held the diary and the papers aloft, and flicked the lighter. The flame jumped up and he held it to the corner of the diary. "The house is next. Time to put you in the basement with the rest of the bodies." He began to laugh uproariously. "You should have seen the looks on that old couple's faces when—"

He didn't get a chance to finish. Just as the flame took hold of the diary and Greta grabbed the bronze candlestick holder, a tall figure ran through the bedroom door and slammed into Michael's back with so much force that he flew into the air and landed in a crumpled heap on the floor.

"Julian!" Greta screamed. "Thank god!" Then she saw the diary on the floor, starting to burn, and she ran over, stomping on it until the flames were extinguished. Once the fire was out, she turned to Julian and threw her arms around him, sobbing. He gathered her into his embrace, and they stood like that for a minute, until Greta regained her composure and pulled away to stare at Michael lying on the floor. "Is he—is he dead?" She realized she was still gripping the candlestick holder, so tightly that the cherubs were cutting into her palm. She dropped it and it landed on the floor with a heavy thud.

Julian leaned over Michael's prone form, breathing hard. "Unfortunately, no. Just unconscious. Glad I played rugby in high school. Never did forget how to make a good tackle. But we have to tie him up or something, just in case. I'll watch him, and you look for rope." Greta nodded and fled down to the kitchen. She pulled open the drawers, not finding any rope, but there was a thick roll of duct tape in one of the cupboards. She brought it back upstairs and handed it to Julian, who deftly tore off a long strip and wrapped it tightly around Michael's wrists. Then he did the same with his ankles.

While he was securing things, Greta finally felt able to speak coherently. "How did you get in? The front door was locked."

Julian laughed. "I know. And I didn't want to knock, signal him that I was here. Remember what I said, that someone could sneak into this place and no one would ever know? That's what I did. I found an old basement access around the side of the house. The lock and hasp were new but the wood was old and rotten. It didn't take much to pull the whole thing off. That basement though—it reeked, like something had died in it. Disgusting."

Greta shivered, remembering what Michael had started to say about the bodies in the basement, and how she had almost been one of them. "Hey," Julian said softly. He stood up and put his arm around her. "It's okay. I'm here, and you're safe. And you are *never* going to a middle-aged psychopath's house without me again, right?"

Greta laughed weakly. "Now, how do we get him into the car? We have to drive into town before we can even call the police."

"Easy. Exactly the same way we carry rugs around in the market." He hoisted Michael, who was groaning slightly, up off the floor and threw him over his shoulder. Greta bent down and picked up the diary. Its edges were crisp and charred, but the majority of it was intact.

"What's that?" Julian asked as they left the room.

"Louisa Duberger's diary. And I can't wait to read it."

🕱   🕱   🕱

"You mean to tell me your fiancé just trussed him up like a Thanksgiving turkey and threw him in the trunk?" Dr. Weldon was dumbfounded. He and Greta were having their first meeting since her encounter with Michael Shepherd, or Michel Duberger, as he turned out to be, and the professor was enthralled at the story she was relating.

Greta inhaled deeply then exhaled. "Yes. There wasn't much else to do—what if he woke up and managed to escape? After everything he'd done, the thought of him out there on the loose was kind of terrifying. I'm so grateful that Julian showed up when he did. Who knows what might have happened to me?"

"Based on what you've already told me, something awful, no doubt. And what about those poor people, the Taylors? What a dreadful thing to happen! If only they had never opened the door to that man."

"I know," Greta agreed, "but we all thought he seemed like a harmless eccentric—at first. According to the police, he killed them almost right away and hid their bodies under a pile of rubble in the back corner of the basement, then basically took over their house. The car he was driving was even registered to them."

"But they still haven't found his wife? I wonder what he did with *her*," Dr. Weldon mused.

"Hopefully nothing. Maybe she just changed her name and she'll reappear now that he's going to jail for a really long time. Or he'll finally confess. The police say he's still refusing to tell them anything." Greta was suddenly weary and sank back into the office chair on the other side of Dr. Weldon's desk.

The professor leaned forward, hands templed under his chin. "So what about the diary? I'd love to take a peek. Are you almost done transcribing it?"

"Close. As soon as I'm finished with it, I'll loan it to you for as long as you like, then it can go to the rare book library, along with the letters. I'm re-transcribing those—Michael's versions were heavily 'sanitized.' The diary makes for pretty tragic reading, following Louisa as she goes from being a carefree young girl to a single mother secretly carrying her brother's child. Incest, rape, murder, drug addiction and recovery—it's got it all. I already have a tentative title for my dissertation. *A Life Under Oak: The Secret World Of Louisa Duberger.*"

"I like it," Dr. Weldon agreed. "A strange and fascinating tale, one I can't wait to find out more about."

"I'd almost believe it was fiction if I hadn't seen the pages with my own eyes. In fact, it's already inspired a couple of prose pieces of my own. I haven't done any creative writing in years, so I owe Louisa for the inspiration. But who would have thought something like that could happen in the Victorian era?"

"Actually," Dr. Weldon said, "it wasn't as uncommon as you think. Brothers and sisters were brought up in pretty close quarters and were often fairly secluded from other people their own age. Usually though, one of them would marry a cousin or another more distant relative, kind of a proxy for the sibling. But with their mother dead and their father incapacitated, there was no one to help poor Louisa."

"I know. I feel terrible for her. What an ordeal to go through on her own in such a short, sad life. At least she had a good relationship with the cousins who took in Louis and she could visit every so often. And those letters that Michael found hidden in the attic—so creepy, so obsessive."

"We can assume they were written by her brother, Lucius?"

"Yes, although none of them were signed. Anyway," she checked the time on her phone, "I need to get going. Julian and I are moving into our new place tomorrow."

Dr. Weldon clapped his hands together in delight. "How exciting for the two of you. I thought things were 'on hold'?"

Greta smiled. "I was worried that they were too, but Julian had other plans. Apparently, he's much better at keeping secrets than me. In fact, the day I went to the rare book library, he was meeting with a real estate agent to help him with the search so that he could surprise me. He found us something perfect, and with my new research assistantship—thank you very much by the way—we can definitely afford it."

"Oh, that's wonderful—my pleasure! But what about your sister, Helen? What will she do?"

"Actually, she's found a job, a proper job. It's strange—once Julian told her what had almost happened to me, it was like a reality check for her. I think Helen realized that with me gone, she had no family left. Family is more important to some people than you might think, as I've discovered lately, and when I got back into town, she and I sat down and had a long conversation; we reconnected in a way I never thought possible. She's really started to straighten herself around—she even talked to my former landlord, Mr. Selensky, and he said she could take over my old room. So I have a lot to do today, what with preparing to move me out and move her in. And I really want to get the last few pages of Louisa's diary finished tonight so I can focus on tomorrow. Funny though."

"What is?"

"The last page of the diary—it just trails off, and it looks like there was a final entry that was torn out."

Dr. Weldon's brow furrowed. "Hmm. Do you think Michael

Shepherd... or Duberger, ripped it out because there was something even worse written on it?"

"Worse than what was already in it? I doubt it. But I'll always wonder what it said."

Louisa: The Last Entry
1899

for now.

Wednesday, February 15th

I have come back from Maison de Lierre, where I had been staying for two months in order to celebrate both Christmas and the occasion of Louis' 7th birthday. He has become quite the little gentleman, with a cheerful and polite disposition that charms us all. He will grow up to be a fine and good man, I am certain of it. Sebastien and Sophie are excellent parents to him—it was the right choice to turn him over to them, and he absolutely dotes on Sophie—indeed, he is quite fixated on her. I watch him, laughing and playing, so innocent and pure, and I am glad that he is happy. For Christmas, he presented me with a poem, one that he said, "I wrote by my own self in English for you, with Mama's help." It was a delightful verse about a windy day:

> *Windy Day for Aunt Louisa*
>
> *What do you do on a windy day*
> *When the wind is pushing you on your way?*

Why, you should quite simply say,
Wind, oh wind, let me play!
Then wind, do as you please,
Take me to fairyland with the breeze
Come now wind, you must be kind.
Don't push so hard, do you mind?

For a child of not quite seven, I thought it a very impressive effort, and it reminded me of my own early attempts at writing, when I was young and full of hope.

My visits to Maison de Lierre were a respite from the life of solitude I lead at Champs Blancs, where Lucius lurks around every corner. He was with me there too, bloody and beckoning, but Louis' laughter managed to keep him at bay to a certain extent. Yet, as much as I enjoyed my time with Louis and the temporary reprieve that it brought, I found I could no longer be among company, joyful or not. The evening before I was due to depart, I informed Sophie and Sebastien that this would be my last visit. I will not return, as miserable as it makes me. They accepted my decision, with a certain amount of relief, I believe, as my presence is a constant reminder of the past—for all of us. Louis is young and will soon forget about me, as children do, and I will become a faint but happy remembrance for him. Prior to departing, I gave Sophie a bound edition of the poetry collection that I had specially printed by a local company last fall. It is the only copy, and I have inscribed it for Louis that he may read the poems when he is older and think of me. The resolution that I have made, of no longer being in his life, fills me with anguish, and in a fit of despair last evening, I tore the pages out of the poetry journal in which I had first penned my dark thoughts and hid them, along with the letters. I should burn them all and be done with it, but they, like Champs Blancs, are a part of my soul and they shall remain together. I have grown used to burying my secrets and they will stay well-hidden, although if this volume, my diary, has been discovered, they may indeed come to light.

The laudanum I put away so many years ago still resides in the locked cupboard and the remains of that bottle are more than enough to ensure my passage from this life into the next once I make the final decision to depart. I will miss Champs Blancs in my own way; however, the beautiful childhood home I once knew has become a loathsome prison and I am a captive of the memories that chain me to it. But before I say farewell to you forever, dear reader, there is something you must know in order that I may meet my maker, or his fiendish counterpart, with a clean conscience. I told you at the beginning of this diary that you would have to decide for yourself what parts were honest and what was fabrication. Perhaps you have guessed it all along; perhaps you have not.

I loved my brother, even after all the terrible things he did. Then why did I kill him? Was I truly in a fugue state with no knowledge of my actions, taking his life even as he cried for my forgiveness? No. Here it is, the plain and simple truth, and it horrifies me to admit it: I murdered Lucius in cold blood. After the encounter that led to the conception of Louis, he sat on the edge of the bed, disgusted with himself. I put a tentative hand on his shoulder but he shoved it away. "No, Louisa. I can no longer look at myself. Or you." With that, he left me alone, my virtue permanently stained. I knew then that my fate was forever entwined with his, that there was no other solution, and I wrote to him, as he had written to me so many times, begging him not to go, pleading with him not to relegate me to a life of solitude. We would stay as we were, Louisa and Lucius, together always, just as we had vowed to each other, just as he had desired. I silently slipped the letter under the door of his chamber and waited for his response. He came to me later, and when I made to embrace him, he stiffened and refused. "No, Louisa. I understand now that I do not love you in the way you desire me to, not truly. My mind has always been a tempest of uncertainty; now I realize that I merely wanted to possess you. If I could have loved anything, it would have been you...but that is not my nature. Champs Blancs, for what it is worth, is yours—I will find my fortune elsewhere."

A daemon possessed me; in desperation and fury, I screamed, "You cannot leave me! Lucius—you made a vow!!"

"Which you broke first. Forgive me, but I must go."

He stood, and as he turned to walk away, I leapt upon him and crushed his skull with the bronze candlestick holder. And how could anyone blame me? He had destroyed my fledgling bond with Tomas before it had a chance to grow, allowed Father to die, ruined me *and* any hope I had of a suitable match, and he did not love me? All of those letters, full of passion and torment, were lies? I could never forgive him, nor forgive myself for believing him, for acquiescing to....

To cover up my own crimes and make it seem as if Lucius truly had abandoned me, I was forced to dispatch the horses. Mabel was an unsuspecting victim of Lucius's derangement—he throttled her when she attempted to leave and fetch Dr. Bain for Father herself—but poor Beechcroft was a victim of mine. He came upon me in the stable as I wept over Jack and Fancy. When I turned, he saw the blood on my hands and clothes and I had no choice. I placed Mabel next to him as she would have wished, their ashes intermingling, together now in both form and spirit. Lucius's body resides at the bottom of the well as I have said; if you look carefully, you will see his face swimming in the dark water. His spirit haunts me day and night and I pray it is a sign that he will love me better in the next life. But I have come to realize that I was always Charybdis, the mythological beast, churning with the madness of the maelstrom, until it devoured me. I pulled everyone into my vortex, visiting the family curse upon them all without their knowledge or even mine. Except for Louis. Never for him. He is the one good thing that came out of our depravity and I pray that he, and all who come after him, may escape it. I leave you with one last thought:

Life's Dream

When I was young, I used to live,

Close by a stream, surrounded

By buttercups and hollyhocks.

On it my hopes were bounded.

My dream it was, to sail that stream,

Until it became a river.

And when the river met the sea,

I'd sail my ship forever.

I'd travel far, to foreign ports,

And fill my ship with treasure.

No stormy seas would set me back,

Nor waves you cannot measure.

But now life's dream is torn apart

With tears instead of motion,

I pray for strength, 'til last I meet,

The vast, far-reaching ocean.

Epilogue: Greta
Four years later.

"You can come in now." The Chair of the Dissertation Committee held the door for Greta and she stepped into the room. The rest of the committee was waiting, stone-faced. She caught Dr. Weldon's eye and he smiled slightly but gave nothing else away. She took her seat at the head of the table and placed her bound thesis in front of her, trying to quell the shaking in her hands. The Chair sat down. "Good afternoon and welcome, Ms. Randall, on behalf of the committee. I hope you've prepared well. We'll ask you to begin with a summary of your dissertation, *Post-Modern Narrative In Victorian Literature: A Study Of The Work Of Louisa Duberger.*"

Greta cleared her throat and stared at the first page of her introduction, the words swimming in front of her eyes. She took a deep breath—she'd been through much worse than this, she admonished herself, and her audience was, while not friendly in appearance, at least interested in what she had to say, if Dr. Weldon hadn't been kidding when he said the buzz about her research was 'palpable.'

"Thank you," she began. "Post-modern narrative is defined by several characteristics, including the unreliable narrator, the use of metafiction, and a profound engagement with intertextuality. In the work of Louisa Duberger, we see all three of these things in play. When I began studying Duberger, I applied a New Criticism approach to her first poetry collection, *Idle Thoughts And Poems*, examining the patterns of natural symbols and metaphors that Duberger employed to create meaning. At the time that I completed my Master's thesis, *Beyond the Garden Gate*, I considered her writing to be fairly typical of the time period in its use of literary devices to establish a relationship between both the natural world and the metaphysical, and had planned to continue my research in the same vein, once again doing a close reading of her second poetry collection. My intention was to draw parallels between those two volumes and the work of other female poets writing at the end of the 19th century. However, I later came to realize, particularly after the discovery of the diary that chronicled Louisa Duberger's life from her eighteenth birthday until the summer of 1892, that Duberger's work was not that of your average female Victorian-era poet, and that there were underlying complexities which lay beyond New Criticism. I then planned on doing a feminist critique of her poetry as it stood in relationship to her diary. But something unexpected happened."

Greta paused and looked up. Her audience was, if not warming to her, attentive—and one or two professors looked almost intrigued. She felt her nerves dissolving, her confidence building, and she continued. "The diary, when it was...rescued, was missing the last entry. It had been torn out. I assumed that the person who had found it, Michel Lucien Duberger, also known as Michael Shepherd, had removed it for his own reasons. He insisted he had not, and was adamant that he knew nothing about what Louisa Duberger may or may not have written on those final pages. Then, two years ago, the property management company who purchased Champs Blancs, the Duberger estate, began an inventory of the house's contents, including several books, one of which was a copy of Homer's *Odyssey*. Tucked inside, between two of the pages in Book Twelve, where Odysseus encounters Charybdis, the monster of the whirlpool, was the last entry from Louisa Duberger's diary. And what was written on those pages threw all my previous thoughts and understanding of Louisa Duberger into chaos—what was true and what was fiction? Was the diary written *as* the tragic events of her life unfolded or was it written after the fact as a metanarrative?... "

Afterwards, Greta sat alone outside the room, waiting for the dissertation committee to make their decision. There had been two rounds of questions and she felt she'd handled them knowledgably and professionally, but there was still uncertainty. Was it enough? She thought about the last two years, the shock of reading those final pages and discovering that Louisa was so much more than Greta had initially believed, not a simple girl who lived a tragically short life, but a complex and clever woman who controlled, if not her own fate, at least the telling of it. She looked at the thick volume in her hands, the work of so many years, and felt immensely proud, regardless of what might happen next. Then the door swung open and Dr. Weldon walked out. He stopped and looked at her seriously, hands in his pockets. "Greta. We're ready for you." She swallowed hard and followed him back into the room, but now, instead of stone-faced silence, the members of the committee were smiling.

The Chair stood and held out her hand. "Congratulations, Dr. Randall. Quite an impressive defense." The rest of the committee came forward and offered their congratulations as well, as Greta tried to maintain her composure. Afterwards, Dr. Weldon invited her back to his office, where he broke into a delighted grin. "Congratulations again, *Doctor* Randall."

Greta exhaled slowly. "Wow. Thank you. For everything— your support, your advice, your kindness—I couldn't have done this without you. How can I ever repay you?"

"The pleasure is completely mine" he answered. "And you've already repaid me—all I ever wanted was for you to solve the mystery of Louisa Duberger, and you did."

Greta laughed sardonically. "But did I? I feel like she's even more of an enigma now than she ever was. For example, if Michael is telling the truth and he didn't hide those last pages himself, then who did? Why would Louisa have written them, and then torn them out and secreted them away? And what about the handwriting? Can we believe Louisa when she said that she and Lucius had almost identical writing styles or—and this is what keeps me up at night—did she write *everything* herself: the poetry, the letters, including the ones she attributes to her brother, the diary, all of it?"

"Interesting premise—if she was the one who wrote everything, what actually happened to her brother?" Dr. Weldon wondered. "Maybe he *wasn't* the true villain in this scenario."

"Who can say? You know, I've studied the census from those years when Louisa was living at Champs Blancs, and the weird thing is that there's no mention of a 'Lucius,' or any brother at all.

Record-keeping from that time period was notoriously spotty—as you've often reminded me, the majority of people back then lived and died in relative anonymity—but there are still more questions than answers, potentially another layer to the narrative. We may never really know," Greta sighed.

Dr. Weldon nodded. "I understand what you mean. But you'll have plenty of time to unravel her even more. The research never stops—publish or perish, as they say, Dr. Randall!"

Greta laughed again, this time genuinely happy. "And to that end, I need to go. Julian is taking me to Champs Blancs Inn And Country House for a second honeymoon, to celebrate. I told him when he booked it that he was jumping the gun, but he'll be happy to know he was right, and so am I—incredibly happy. I can't wait to see what the property management company has done with the place. I hear it's getting five-star reviews and it's only been open for a month."

"I wonder if they'll let you pull up any floorboards," Dr. Weldon mused, then winked. "Maybe you'll find something that turns all your research on its head once again!"

"I seriously hope not!" Greta exclaimed. "I've had enough twists and turns for a lifetime."

Julian drove down the newly paved laneway towards Champs Blancs Inn and Country House. "I can't believe how much it's changed," he said. "They did an incredible job bringing this place back to life."

"It's gorgeous," Greta agreed, admiring the freshly re-slated roof and the flower gardens flanking the impressive entryway. "Do you remember how run-down it was the last time we were here? What a difference."

"Are you sure you'll be okay? No flashbacks or anything?"

"No, I'm fine. I think knowing that Michael Shepherd is safely in prison helps. Hard to believe he honestly thought that he could turn this place into a famous destination and no one would figure out who he was. Then again, he *is* a narcissistic sociopath." She sighed. "I just wish Helen could have come with us. Maybe next time." Greta looked at her phone. Full bars. Obviously, the new owners had no problem getting a cell signal in the valley.

"Stop obsessing," Julian chided her. "Helen will call as soon as her accounting exam is done, and then the two of you can rehash it. I'm sure she'll pass with flying colours, and that promotion is in the bag."

Greta sighed and tucked her phone away. She caught sight of the new coach house, built using the stable's original stone foundation, and had to force herself not to think about what Louisa had done—or at least what she'd said she had done. Who knew how much of her story was true? All of it? Or none of it? As they passed the old wellhead, topped now with a huge urn of flowers, Greta frowned. "Did it say anything on the Champs Blancs website about historical interpretation? You know, like actors

198

dressed as characters from the Victorian period?"

"No, why? Did you see someone? That'd be kind of cool."

Greta looked at Julian and smiled, then turned back to the well. But the two children, the boy and girl wearing old-fashioned clothing that she'd seen standing in front of it a moment ago, holding hands, were gone.

Suzanne Craig - Whytock
About the Author.

Award-winning writer Suzanne Craig-Whytock is the author of four previous novels, *Smile, The Dome, The Seventh Devil*, and *The Devil You Know*, and two short story collections, *Feasting Upon The Bones* and *At The End Of It All*, as well as the humour collection *What Any Normal Person Would Do.*

Her short fiction and poetry have appeared in numerous literary journals, and she regularly publishes essays focused on life's absurdities under the pen name 'Mydangblog.' She is also the Editor of DarkWinter Literary Magazine, an online journal which publishes short stories and poetry from both emerging and established writers, as well as the founder of DarkWinter Press and Baxter House Editions. *Charybdis* is her fifth novel.